MAX EGREMONT

Max Egremont was born in 1948 and educated at Eton and Oxford. He has written two biographical studies, THE COUSINS and BALFOUR, and three novels, THE LADIES' MAN, DEAR SHADOWS and PAINTED LIVES. He lives in West Sussex with his wife and four children.

'This novel is a remarkable achievement. Not only has Max Egremont successfully imagined a woman's most secret thoughts – an ambitious attempt in itself – but he has also evoked a curious haunting atmosphere . . . I was immensely impressed by PAINTED LIVES. It leaves one with a sensation of limbo, and it will not be easily forgotten. The finely wrought plot, the fragile and so delicate development of the characters and the excellence of Max Egremont's prose lead to a bitter-sweet result that is triumphant'
Sarah Sackville-West in The Catholic Herald

'The story-told-backwards at its best . . . Egremont counterpoints the aridness of the male characters with the heroine's turbulence and maintains a masterly tempo throughout'
Max Davidson in the Daily Telegraph

Max Egremont

PAINTED LIVES

First published in Great Britain in 1989 by Hamish Hamilton Ltd.

Sceptre edition 1990

Sceptre is an imprint of Hodder and Stoughton Paperbacks, a division of Hodder and Stoughton Ltd.

British Library C.I.P.

Egremont, Max, *1948–*
　Painted lives.
　I. Title
　823'.914[F]

ISBN 0-340-53093-6

Printed and bound in Great Britain for Hodder and Stoughton Paperbacks, a division of Hodder and Stoughton Ltd., Mill Road, Dunton Green, Sevenoaks, Kent TN13 2YA. (Editorial Office: 47 Bedford Square, London WC1B 3DP) by Clays Ltd., St Ives plc.

For Francis Wyndham

CHAPTER ONE

THE HOUSE IS ISOLATED, AT THE END OF A LONG DRIVE. For most of its history, Cragham was known as a castle but the last three generations of the family who live there have preferred to call it a house, so that is the term we will use in these pages. The ancestor of the present owner built fortifications in 1334. In the seventeenth century another ancestor transformed the castle into a mansion and some of the rooms date from this time.

The family became rich. Beneath the land were deposits of coal and with the nineteenth century came a wish to live in a grander style. An owner of the house was made Viceroy of India. He summoned an architect who made additions to Cragham of a mediaeval character, additions that were to be cursed by succeeding generations for the way they added to the cost of running the house. In his retirement, he decorated a small room off the hall with tiles in the Mogul fashion and would sit here sometimes on summer evenings, surrounded by mementoes of his days of eastern splendour, while his wife read aloud from translations of Indian love lyrics. They were a childless couple and it was said that time hung heavily upon them towards the end.

The Viceroy had been created an earl. As he had no sons, the title became extinct with his death. The property passed to a brother who was vague and feckless. Both he and his heir, father of the present owner, were forced to sell land at low prices to pay debts. The property dwindled and the older inhabitants of the area began to look back to the days of the house's vanished glory. But the family remained, determined to cling to the place as long as possible, for it was their home.

The present owner, like his predecessors, is called Layburn. Last year his seventieth birthday passed without celebration, in spite of his oldest son's suggestion that they should make something of it. Since his wife's death, some twenty years ago, he has led a quiet life. Circumstances have forced him to turn parts of the Victorian additions to the house into three flats for retired couples. He tries to see as little of these people as possible and has been known to hide behind trees in order to avoid them in the garden or park where he likes to work among the shrubs and plants: also to pursue his lifelong interest in the birds and animals that live in this corner of northern England.

This evening Layburn has a guest, a man of his own age.

They sit in the drawing room, their chairs on either side of a large chimney piece of white and brown marble. In the fireplace a log flares gently; it is November and fires are needed to fight the cold.

Layburn is tall and thin with a face like a bird of prey and a head of thick grey hair. At his feet lie two black dogs, curled up against each other. He pulls back a sleeve of the jacket of his dark blue suit to uncover a watch and arches his thin wrist as he peers at the dial. For his age he has good eyes.

'He's late,' he says.

They are waiting for a young man who is coming from London to attend to the pictures that hang in the house. The guest smiles. He is a round man of medium height with a bald pink head and wisps of thin white hair.

'He'll be nervous, Bob. And there may be train trouble. When I came up there was a rumour...'

Layburn interrupts. 'He's coming by car. And there may be snow tonight. Did you listen to the news?' The voice is deep, with a hint of melancholy or regret: sad yet strong.

Philip Bligh, the guest, laughs. He knows his host well and likes to see the autocrat revealed.

'Snow in November? Surely not. In any case I'm afraid I have no wireless.'

'Not even in London?'

Bligh speaks slowly, for Layburn is rather deaf now. 'I do have one in London,' he says, then a piece of phlegm sticks in his throat and he coughs, lowering his reddening face towards his chest and covering his mouth with one hand.

'The ground was white with frost this morning,' Layburn says.

Bligh controls himself at last. ' "Now hung with pearls, the dropping trees appear...," ' he begins, his quick, high word slightly constricted.

'What?' Layburn speaks louder.

' "Their faded honours scattered on her bier." ' The couplet completed, Bligh coughs twice and the phlegm goes. 'We must try to be as welcoming as possible,' he shouts.

'But of course,' Layburn says. 'Why not?'

George Loftus drives slowly along the streets of a large town. He has a feeling that he has taken the wrong turning, that there must be a road which avoids the crowded centre.

He has a dark blue van instead of a car because he needs to carry pictures from one place to another. The van's engine is noisy, its interior bleak. George does not like this, for he is a neat person but the vehicle's age is against him in his struggles to keep it clean.

He drives down a broad thoroughfare, trying to observe

the passing scene through the darkness. George prides himself that he can see beauty not only in the obvious symmetry of great art or landscape, but in certain lights and shades, certain haphazard forms. The way shadows fall, the pattern of trees or buildings, a distant view of a housing estate on the outskirts of a city, blocks rising towards an evening sky, the onward sweep of a highway: to all these he tries to respond with sympathy, with awe. Few things are, he thinks, wholly ugly or bad.

He changes gear to slow down for a set of traffic lights and the van's engine rises into a grinding roar which reminds him of the rasping tones of Dr Herbert Friedrich, director of the Institute. Friedrich, his master, has told him about this task which involves a long journey north.

This was a good opportunity, Friedrich had said. 'The pictures do not sound as if they are of outstanding quality. Major Layburn mentions an eighteenth-century sporting scene, a small Dutch landscape, an Italian religious group and a modern portrait. He does not say what their condition is, but I imagine he will want only surface work. If there is more to be done, you will have to bring them back to London with you. I do not know this major. He must have dealt with Kirk in the past. Someone told me that Philip Bligh was involved – but I have not had time to ask him. Old Bligh! In any case it was a long time ago. I will tell the Major to expect you. You should take your winter woollies!'

Friedrich's laugh is loud, embarrassing in public places. George wishes he could like the man for he has so many admirable qualities: his professionalism, the courage to take risks, a dislike of the smart, a determination to promote the cause of the Institute and its works. Yes, all these are good and Friedrich is not a dreamer. Yet this is probably where things begin to go wrong between them. Friedrich's coldness chills him, even though George wishes to disregard it, even though he tries to forget that works of art almost certainly mean little to the doctor outside an academic analysis of their

4

historical and technical worth. No, Friedrich might well have chosen accountancy, banking or the law as his career. At the Institute, he has shown himself to be a good administrator. The place runs more smoothly than ever before; even the oldest member of staff admits this. Yet what does the permanent collection mean to Friedrich, who sees everything in terms of points in favour and points against? Always his summing up is admirably judicious, unanswerable. There are no loose ends. George lifts one hand off the steering wheel to fling his hair back from his forehead. He knows that Friedrich does not feel. To think and to feel: he is sure this is the best combination and Friedrich merely calculates. In consequence, Friedrich sees nothing but the obvious result, the correct calculation. Here, for instance: here the man would offer mere polite interest and a series of precise but sterile comparisons.

So, at the traffic lights, George Loftus looks to his right in search of beauty. Through the cold fog rise the outlines of Victorian development, a row of shop windows, some brightly lit, others with blackened interiors; then a large block towering above its surroundings. Across the front of this, in high blue and white neon letters, is the familiar name of an insurance company. Now, he wonders, what about this? The shapes in the fog, the dim side streets that snake off into tunnels of night formed by lines of distantly vanishing orange lights. He thinks of Doré, of Lowry, of the city as a great pounding heart.

'You're a romantic, George,' Mrs Kirk has often told him: Mrs Kirk the widow of Geoffrey Kirk, Dr Friedrich's predecessor as director; Mrs Kirk in whose large Hampstead house he lodges. With Mrs Kirk he talks often of the Institute, of his work, happy to act as a link between this old woman and her dead husband, a man who apparently never strayed from the most upright conduct. Often too he finds himself smiling slightly as once again she arrives at her favourite theme of decline, the growth of greed and careerism, the triumph of the hideous: the sound of the barbarians at the gate.

He has spoken to her about this new assignment and Mrs Kirk remembers the Layburn family, although she has never been to their great house in the North. At first she seemed a little annoyed that Friedrich, whom she despises, should have become involved in yet another part of the world where she and Geoffrey had once moved.

'Friedrich gave you this job?' she asked, her voice harsh in the badly lit Hampstead living room that is crowded with furniture. Beside her chair, a cat raised its head to look briefly at her long austere lined face. 'How could he know ... ?' She glanced down at her thin hands where bones show like a pattern of dry sticks. 'I suppose Philip Bligh is still the link with that collection. Does Philip ever come to the Institute now, I wonder?'

George said that he had never met Bligh. Mrs Kirk went on. 'He retired about five years ago, just before Geoffrey died. He never made any effort to keep in touch, after he left. And Geoffrey had always been kind to Philip, although I know he thought him a bit of a dabbler: not quite as careful as he should have been in his work. Poor Philip. How he loved the Layburns. Geoffrey and I used to laugh at the way he kept bringing them into the conversation – Bob and Catherine this, Bob and Catherine that. His great excuse was the collection – but when we asked him about the pictures he had to admit they weren't really of great quality: anyway not enough for Geoffrey to make a special journey north.'

Her voice dropped, short of breath: the frustration and tiredness of age. 'When are you going? Philip brought the Layburns to the Institute several times, for exhibitions or concerts. How beautiful they were, both of them!' Mrs Kirk smiled. 'Young and beautiful. Of course I had heard of the family and its history. He had been a hero in the war, or so Philip told us. That was when they had first met, Philip and Major Layburn. The war always seemed important to Philip.

Perhaps there had been some incident in the desert: I don't know. But usually she came alone, with Philip. I spoke to her once for some time, I remember. She seemed so eager to learn, her wonderful face creased in a frown as she listened to what Geoffrey said. Then she died – a year or two afterwards, Philip told us. He seemed upset: some rare disease of the blood. I dare say he still goes there, to the house. They were important to Philip: the Layburns. And I'm sure the pictures are interesting. You will remember it all, won't you? I want to hear.'

He drives on and the buildings thin out into suburban neatness. Soon the lights end, to mark the beginnings of the country. Most of the mines have closed in this area and much of it has been restored to a pre-industrial state. Here the darkness and fog hide an imagined Arcadia.

CHAPTER TWO

THE HOUSE IS LARGE AND BADLY LIT. HE HAS expected this.

A frail elderly woman dressed in black takes him to the top floor. She walks with a slight limp, wheezes and puffs on the broad wooden stairs and stops twice for a short time to rest before they reach a small, white-walled bedroom. The room is cold: bare, except for a narrow bed with a white iron bedstead, a wooden cupboard, a small table beside the bed and a hard chair. The curtains have not been drawn. Through the darkness outside two lights burn in the distance: houses on the edge of the park.

Along the passage is a bathroom, painted a dull shade of cream. Here she leaves him for a few minutes, having asked if he wishes 'to wash his hands' before he follows her down the stairs again to the panelled drawing room and the two old men. Both stand when he enters and, in their presence, he has only a moment to take in the high ceiling, the dark panelling, the tall gilt pier-glass over the chimney piece: the slightly smoking fire, the seventeenth-century portraits in two rows on the walls, the long-faded red curtains hanging from carved pelmet boards above two high windows; then, beside the door, the best picture in the house (or so his researches have told him), the great sporting scene of horses, riders and hounds in a wooded landscape.

Major Layburn waits with his thin hand held out, his eyes like twin orbs of bright glass.

'You've come from London?' The handshake is brief and hard. The dogs do not stir beside Layburn's shoes which have been polished a brilliant black.

'Yes. I'm so sorry...'

'They're supposed to have improved the road.' Layburn sighs, the low voice strong, almost melodic. Suddenly he smiles and the lines of his face leap as if shocked by this odd benevolence. 'Have you seen your room? Then have a drink.' He points to a line of bottles and glasses on a table under a portrait of a woman in a blue dress trimmed with lace. 'Why don't you help yourself?'

George pours out a large measure of whisky, quickly takes a gulp, almost retches as the fiery liquid attacks his throat and bursts its way into his system. He turns, confused, to realise that Layburn and the other man are now standing beside the fire. 'I'm sorry,' Layburn says. 'I didn't introduce you. Philip Bligh. Mr ..?' He stares at the boy.

'Loftus. George Loftus.'

Bligh smiles. His small nose and amused lips have a delicate shape. 'I do hope your journey wasn't too unpleasant.'

Layburn interrupts. 'Perhaps we should go in to dinner,' he says brusquely. 'They've been waiting for over an hour.'

The Cragham Hunt. This is the name of the picture he has seen reproduced in books and articles. He has been struck always by the elegance of the scene: that and the curiously exotic quality the artist has managed to give to the landscape which makes it more redolent of the South – perhaps Tuscany or Umbria – than of England. Yet it passes as a representation of the Layburn of the day with his hounds and a few of his hunting friends. As such, George thinks that the artist has left a piece of the immortal past, deathless as long as this picture survives.

The artist is unknown. There have been guesses. Whenever it is exhibited someone presses the case for a particular name, but the arguments run up against a lack of documentary evidence. Scholars agree only that the scene can be described as Augustan, from a period of elegance, purity and refinement.

Yes, it is great work. He glances again at the vast picture. Then, looking closer, again quickly, for he knows these old men must want their dinner, he sees that the round faces of the riders are inhuman masks, their features lifeless against the grace of their shapes and costume; the horses have more animation, more sign of life, and it is the view of the great stretch of country, the woods blending into fields, green beneath a pale sky ribbed with bands of thin cloud, the hounds and horses and men bright in the foreground – it is this which lifts the picture above the crudeness of its individual parts.

Long and narrow, the dining room is darker than the room they have left, lit only by lights above pictures (again portraits and also one large landscape, probably Dutch). Layburn sits at the head of the polished oval wooden table, facing a window covered with long pink curtains, the colour of which blends with the grey walls. On a sideboard near the window is a bowl of four or five apples, some of them brown with decay, beginning to rot.

They are served by the same elderly woman who stumbles occasionally as she makes her way round the table. George is on Layburn's left, Bligh on their host's right: an order of precedence founded on age.

'How long have you been at the Harman Institute?' Bligh's question is friendly.

'Three years.'

Bligh clears his throat and starts to speak, the emphasis falling on certain words in rapid succession. 'I worked there you know, until my retirement five years ago. Are you fond of the old place? Now there's a story that casts considerable credit on this country for a change: evidence of a rare triumph over the philistines. Do you remember how it all started, how Alfred Harman left most of his great mining fortune and art collection to the nation, to establish a gallery and institute for the study of art in his huge Victorian town house? Of course, the building is a monstrosity in a way.' Bligh smiles, shrugs his shoulders. 'Do you remember it, Bob?'

'Yes,' says Layburn. 'I do.'

Bligh turns to George Loftus. 'You work with Herbert Friedrich?'

'In the conservation department. Did...?'

'I scarcely knew him. When I was there he was still up in Leeds. It was an interesting appointment. Of course, Geoffrey Kirk, the Director in my day, was a different type altogether. I should imagine the place has become rather more austere. More contemporary as well. For instance, there was that exhibition of modern sculpture...'

'It attracted attention,' George says.

'Oh, I'm sure it did. And Friedrich showed courage in staging it, in view of the present clamour against such work. Perhaps Geoffrey was too unwilling to take risks. You see he refused to go against the demands of his own taste and standards. He had immense knowledge: really immense knowledge – particularly of the French seventeenth and eighteenth centuries.' Bligh pauses and lifts his hands in a gesture of regret. 'But his books are disappointing. Too specialised. Too obscure. He once told me that he had read a lot of German in his youth and feared that it may have affected his style. The lectures were much better. Almost a performance: the pauses, the use of drama or theatre. Here one saw the great burning light of enthusiasm, of love for his subject. To meet he seemed shy, almost absurdly modest: a charming but diffident man. But occasionally the steel showed – especially in committee, for Geoffrey would never compromise if he believed strongly in something or someone. He was an admirable man: not easy to know well.'

'I live with Mrs Kirk,' George says.

'Mary? Not in sin, I hope?' Bligh laughs. Layburn does not laugh.

'No, no. I am her lodger. Since the Professor's death, she has taken in a student from the Institute, to have someone with her in the house.'

'And how is Mary?' Bligh's voice takes on a note of pity.

'Her mind is completely alert. But she suffers from arthritis, particularly in the knees.'

Bligh turns to Layburn. 'Your complaint, Bob. Do you get it there as well?'

'A little.'

He looks again at George Loftus. 'Tell me, were there any children? I can't remember.'

'One son, who lives in America.'

'Most of her friends must be dead so she is alone, apart from you that is. Does she ever go out? For instance, if I were to ask her to dinner in my flat – a quiet evening, you understand – would she come? I could try to get hold of some people who were at the Institute in Geoffrey's day.'

'I'm sure she would be most grateful, Philip,' Layburn says.

Bligh's smile is uncertain. 'I will try.'

Briefly George Loftus pays no attention, for he is becoming aware of the house in a way that has not been possible before. His arrival, the journey upstairs with the woman in black to the gloom of the white bedroom and forlorn atmosphere of the abandoned attic floor, the return to this half-lit grandeur: these impressions have followed one another in a succession of swiftly crumbling images. Now he looks carefully and tries to remember about the family: the two generals, one who had fought with Marlborough, the other with Wellington: then the Viceroy – these were men who had shaped history. The house is their temple and its present owner has followed them by becoming a hero in battle himself, or so Mrs Kirk had said. What a mixture it is, a reflection of different times and fashions. These rooms on the ground floor are seventeenth century. The hall, with its absurd carved heraldic portraits on either side of the chimney piece, must (he knows from his reading of Pevsner) date from the time of the Victorian improvements.

Then he checks himself. He must not be fooled by this place, for what is the reality: a round, red-faced man talking of days that are gone, of the dead and those who are barely alive? Bligh is waiting. He must play his part in the conversation. 'I hardly knew Professor Kirk. He interviewed me for my position at the Institute but by the time I came to work there he had died. It was all quite quick.'

'Mercifully so,' Bligh says. 'You would have liked him. And now people are beginning to forget. The other day I saw an interview with Herbert Friedrich in some paper where he said he felt the Institute should be made "more accessible". Really! Of course, this was precisely what Geoffrey did when he started those concerts. Do they have concerts there now?'

'Occasionally.'

'In our day there were two or three a week in summer.' He looks at Layburn. 'Once I took Catherine to a programme of Schubert. Do you remember?'

'Yes,' Layburn says. 'She liked music.'

After dinner they return to the drawing room, followed by the dogs, Layburn and Bligh to sit in armchairs on either side of the slightly smoking fire, with George in another chair on the same side of the room as Bligh, separated from his fellow guest by a carved table on which rests a plant in a china pot and a copy of *The Field*.

Bligh joins his hands together across the hump of his stomach; his chest rises and falls in time to his regular, slow breathing and his eyes are closed. Is he asleep? Then Layburn's voice, firm above the crackling of the burning wood, makes the hands flutter apart, the long slow breaths quicken.

'Shall we listen to the news?'

Their host reaches across to a small radio set on the carved table and presses a button. A loud voice fills the room for half an hour. 'The Government today announced its plans for the reform of secondary education . . .' Eventually Layburn's hand moves towards the machine when it is announced that the next programme is to be an episode in a weekly history of the European Community, or Common Market, 'as it is more widely known'.

The silence returns. Then Layburn speaks quietly.

'Did they tell you the sort of thing we want done?'

'Dr Friedrich mentioned one or two possibilities.'

'It's for my son, really,' Layburn goes on, then looks towards Bligh. 'Charles.' Bligh nods, puts his hands back so that once more they are resting on the small hill above his waist. 'For Charles,' Layburn repeats. 'I'll show you the pictures in the morning.'

'What pictures are these, Bob?' Bligh asks. 'The Lawrence in the red passage of the General? The Viceregal portraits? The hunt?'

'No,' Layburn says. 'Not the hunt.'

'A fascinating work,' Bligh says. 'A huge depiction of the Cragham Hunt, only a few miles away from this house. Catherine wanted to find the precise place.'

Layburn interrupts. 'No stretch of country in this part of the world can ever have looked like that.'

Bligh laughs. 'Oh, I know. But it may be possible to seek

out what one might call the original contours. The artist may have based his flight of fancy on fact. Indeed, Catherine once imagined that she had identified . . .'

Layburn breaks in once more. 'I know that place. You can't see anything: only Fairfield colliery, the new housing estate and then the coast. Surely she can't have been thinking of the moors on the other side.'

George tries to help. 'It can be difficult to recognise an eighteenth-century landscape now. Trees have grown up or have been cut down. Towns have expanded, new methods of agriculture developed.'

'The contours have surely remained the same,' Bligh says. 'This country has escaped a major earthquake. No tidal waves have thundered in from the North Sea.'

Layburn sighs. 'We should go to bed,' he murmurs, and looks at his young visitor. 'Did Beryl show you to your room?'

'Beryl?'

'The thin woman in black,' Bligh says.

'Oh yes. Thank you.'

Layburn stands. 'Breakfast is at half-past eight in the dining room. I hope you sleep well.'

CHAPTER THREE

IN THE WHITE BEDROOM, THE THICK FLOWERED
curtains have been drawn.

George undresses quickly and climbs into bed. He has
forgotten to pack any pyjamas, so wears his shirt to have
some protection against the chill air. Beneath his thin body
the mattress feels pleasantly soft; as he turns there is the sound
of accommodating springs, even a slight bounce to the way
that he is raised instantly to a new position. The bedside
light leaves the rest of the room in shadow, dulls the white
of the walls and blurs the two pictures, both prints: one over
the fireplace of a cavalry charge at the Battle of Waterloo,
the other (on the wall opposite) an ancient map of the county
with the larger towns marked in feint script.

Lying in bed with the light still on, he knows that he has
two choices: the first is to read *The Return of the Native* by
Thomas Hardy, the book he has brought with him, the
second to turn out the light and wait for his mind to be
filled with ideas of Pat, the receptionist at the Institute.

Pat. Cheerful Pat with her red hair that he sometimes
imagines is on fire in the sun. With Pat there is fire and ice,
the fire of his own feelings and the ice of her response, of
her perpetual good manners he has come to hate. Always
she has a cheerful word or smile for everyone: George, Dr
Friedrich, the rest of the Institute's staff: she waves and grins
at them all from behind the desk where she sits with her

telephone equipment and lists of the numbers of the extensions or the people who have appointments in the building. In summer he can scarcely bear to look at her when she wears a dress or a blouse which shows her plump bare arms and slightly freckled flesh, her long bare legs.

He has two lives with Pat. One consists of the truth: that he has never touched her, has never been to her flat in Swiss Cottage where she lives with three other girls, has only managed to persuade her three times to sit with him at lunch in the Institute's restaurant, once to come to the pub after work, once also to walk with him in Hyde Park when she let loose an astonishing cascade of talk. Astonishing? No, not really – but there had been so much of it: about her family in East Acton, her aunt's hip operation, one of the girls in the flat who spent too much time on the telephone to a man who lived in Glasgow, a man made pathetic in Pat's eyes by his size and the spots on his face, a small man not worth the cost of these telephone calls. 'Why does she do it?' Pat cried out in a voice so loud that another couple in the park had turned to look at her, the woman briefly withdrawing her arm from her lover's shoulder. Or was he her lover? George did not know but assumed he was, that everyone was enjoying the fullest possible relations with each other in these easy times.

That afternoon he winced not only at the sight of others together when he was alone but also at Pat's contempt for the small man from Glasgow, for he too is small, or 'short', as she said. Why does he want women taller than he is? Yet so few people are smaller, so few that the limited choice would force even greater frustrations upon him. So he gives into the force that draws him to Pat, that makes him listen to her views on everything from the filth on the streets of East Acton to the great Friedrich himself, whom she likes because he is always so polite, always has time for a word or a smile. 'I've got a soft spot for the Doctor,' Pat said once. 'He seems too good for this world somehow, doesn't he?

And sometimes, in the mornings, he looks so tired – as if someone had dragged him out of bed. I'm glad that you and Dr Friedrich get along so well. It's nice to see people working together. You're a bit of an outsider, aren't you, George? A bit of a lone wolf.'

She is right. He is on the edge of life, not only at the Institute but wherever he finds himself. In bed he smiles, deriving a curious strength from this knowledge of an existence apart. Pat had said Friedrich was 'too good for this world', perhaps implying that she believed George to be the same. But what would she say if she knew of his second life with her, a life of the imagination where ice is dissolved by fire? In this, Pat's words are only those of surrender, words changing quickly to the soft cries of a new dream. Pat before him, perhaps on some huge bed or the grass of a great empty field where the soft turf gives way easily beneath them; or in the ruins of a Gothic abbey, huge decorated stones half buried beneath a tangle of ivy and weeds, the tumbled pillars and capitals symbolic of the dead ideals which litter his life – but not only here (he hopes) as a victim of his wishes, also on a hill above the rest of the world, the bright figure of mysterious feminine power.

So he tries to think of her not as Pat who smiles at everyone from behind her desk at the Institute, the Pat who believes Dr Friedrich to be 'too good for this world', but as a force known also to those grand possessors of his respect and awe: the great artists who leave these golden trails for their disciples. 'Do not use the word "vision",' Friedrich has told him. 'It is too loose, too sloppy. Too ill defined.' But he comes back to it again and again in his mind: the vision of youth, of beauty, of an ideal coming to him from the works in the Institute's permanent collection, from the white stone of the classical figures in the sculpture gallery, from his dreams of Pat.

'What can you tell us about the Rembrandt, George?' Friedrich once asked him in front of one of the Institute's greatest pictures, a portrait of an old man. 'Now, no visions please!'

They were with an American from Chicago, the director of a foundation Friedrich hoped to persuade to fund an extension of the conservation department. He had started to answer, something about the Jewish or biblical context of the work, when Friedrich interrupted. 'No, no! Dr Strauss knows all that. We are not dealing with a first-year student!' The laugh followed, so loud this time that people turned to look and a terrified child was rushed away by its mother. 'Tell us about the way you would treat the picture. Look there, at the discoloration at the top and on the left cheek. What caused that? Please...' and once more the laugh.

Then, of course, he gave the technical details about the overpainting, the previous work done by a restorer in the last century and the way that the recent additions had faded into a different shade to the original colour. Almost, he had added, what struck him most about the work: its truth and simplicity, the ability to strike through the intellect to some bare fact of existence. The Pat of his dreams is the same, with the same roots of feeling and power: an idea, yes, but a felt need, and for a moment he had thought of saying, 'Dr Strauss, Dr Friedrich, let me explain. On your way out you may see a girl with red hair at the desk by the telephone switchboard. I think about her more than any picture, any work of art, these days. Is this right! Say yes – because the root of it all is the same, isn't it? That simplicity. That love.'

He will never speak this way, he knows, as long as he depends upon Friedrich's goodwill for his job. For he enjoys his work at the Institute and is pleased with the leap he has made from the world created by his parents in their house on the outskirts of a small East Anglian town: the world of his father's departure for work each morning at the large ironmonger's shop, his mother's unrealistic view of his talents, the daily encounters with various old school friends who did not go to university and now have jobs in the canning factory or one of the other businesses on the new industrial estate.

Mr Loftus's worry about his son's prospects made him speak often of the attractions of ironmongery. Mr Loftus started at the age of sixteen, worked his way up to manager; then on the death of the bachelor Mr Timson, the last member of the founding family, inherited the business. The shop continued to be called Timson's. The business had grown. Under Mr Loftus, the DIY side strengthened and Timson's had a reputation throughout Norfolk, Suffolk and northern Essex. The only problem, as George heard frequently, was parking. The shop was in the centre of the town, ideally placed, of course, in Mr Timson's day. Now the narrow streets and neat market square were overrun with cars. Mr Loftus knew that he lost business because of this. Then there was another threat, potentially much more damaging: the local council's plan to turn large parts of the town into a pedestrian precinct, thereby isolating shops in the centre from any traffic at all.

In George's last year at the University, there were fatherly hints that it was time to think about work. Mr Loftus looked no longer with such interest at his son's sketches of some nearby church or monument. Now these were brushed to one side, to the sadness of the boy's mother, and the conversation returned to the shop, the threat of the pedestrian precinct or evidence that people were favouring the large discount store recently opened some ten miles away where there was free parking and a wider choice of goods.

A new tension entered the house. That summer, the sun seemed to burn into him and day after day the flat lands around the town shimmered under a vast pale blue sky. George would rise early, unlock his bicycle, put his paints and sketching pad into a satchel and ride out to the country-side, away from the atmosphere of threat and anxiety. 'What are you going to live off?' The cry, accompanied generally by a thump as Mr Loftus's large pale fist hit the arm of the chair, would ring through the rooms of the house, bought after years of toil in the threatened shop.

At that time there were only two hours in the week when the family was at ease together. The summer, in addition to being one of the hottest and driest on record, had also seen two costume dramas repeated on television, on Monday and Thursday evenings: one the story of the life and love affairs of Byron, the other the saga of a family of Yorkshire mill owners which stretched from the industrial revolution to the start of the Second World War. So on Mondays and Thursdays, after supper, the three Loftuses had sat down in front of their set. Mrs Loftus preferred Byron: Mr Loftus the mill owners, stirring agitatedly in his seat as the Luddities smashed new machinery or several hundred men were thrown out of work at the start of the Depression of the 1930s. George valued the hours more for the serenity they brought to the household, a serenity deepened by the fact that the programmes were repeats of episodes his parents had seen before. Mr and Mrs Loftus seemed soothed by their knowledge of what would happen next. Often one of them would anticipate a line of dialogue or nod with delight at a particularly vivid or apt turn of the drama.

He loves his parents. Sometimes when his mother speaks in a way which takes him back to that childhood feeling of love and trust, he finds himself wishing he might never leave her: once, for instance, when she described a display of flowers in the town's public park – 'And such marigolds, such marigolds', her voice trailing off into a silent remembrance of beauty. He is sure that she feels this more than anyone he can imagine and the feeling is so right, so true, purer than the simplest line, colour or word can express. Yet he has to leave. What can he say to her now while he watches and listens for another of these tender moments? No, there is nothing left but glimpses of wonder: these and his father's angry impatience.

He turns in his bed again. The job at the Institute had

taken him away from a cramped life in the cold ugly town of his childhood. It had come naturally out of his university degree in the History of Art which set him further apart from the ironmonger's shop and fears of the pedestrian precinct. He was to be trained as a restorer. On the day of the interview Geoffrey Kirk, then the director, had shown him out, past the receptionist's desk, through the door into Great Hall. Had Pat been there, behind the switchboard, to smile at this small, serious youth?

He turns out the light and wishes he could remember. At any rate she is with him now in the narrow bed in this cold room, so he takes her in slowly, starting at her neck, moving down to her breasts where she responds with a sigh and a slight twist of her body. 'No, this way,' he murmurs and she comes back, for they have much to do together before the end of the night.

On the floor below in another bedroom, a larger, colder room with pale green painted panelling, Philip Bligh lies on the verge of sleep.

In his mind he too is not alone but back in the desert in an armoured car that is on fire, the flames rushing towards him as he tries to escape: then suddenly a new light comes with the opening of the hatch, hands reach down to grip under his shoulders and pull him towards the day and a huge cloudless sky. He looks up, smiles to see Bob Layburn, his saviour, the man to whom he must now give everything: his life, his loyalty, his trust. 'My shirt,' he whispers, 'it's burning,' and he looks at the thin khaki, grits his teeth as they lie together on the roof of the vehicle and Bob quickly beats out the flames, the blows bringing not pain but the prospect of endless relief. 'Wait here,' Bob says. 'We must wait. The others were moving forward when you were hit. Just a reconnaissance exercise. They'll be back. Stay here with me now and rest for a while.'

Had this happened? No. But it is one of the ways he tries to imagine himself alone with Bob, at last a friend in the true but guiltless sense. He supposes these will continue to come to him until the end of his life: these and the idea that things might have been better with Catherine if she had lived.

CHAPTER FOUR

'Surely among a rich man's flowering lawns . . .'

Bligh remembers the line as he looks out of his bedroom window the next morning, towards the grass and the trees of the park. The day is grey, without colour or light, the sun hidden.

This house has played a large part in Bligh's life. He has taken the trouble to learn about its history and its inhabitants, the two generals, the Viceroy, Bob's spendthrift grandfather. Some were distinguished, or so it seemed — although he wonders how much their achievements were made easier by the times in which they had flourished, when men in their position were thought to have a natural right to rule. He knows many of the references to them in the published diaries and letters of their contemporaries and someone has recently written a life of the Viceroy which makes large claims for him. *Layburn: An Imperial Statesman*, it is called. Bligh smiles. These men are not for him. He imagines their rough habit of command, their arrogance and coarse appetite for pleasure. In spite of his apparent stiffness and dignity the Viceroy had had a long retinue of mistresses, including a notorious courtesan to whom he had brought his own strong brand of Russian tea for their late afternoon assignations at her house off Park Lane.

Bligh likes to read about them. He likes to imagine the

Viceroy almost exploding out of his stiff shirt and high collar as the courtesan flutters her eyelashes, the pomposity falling away as he pursues her into the bedroom and starts to fiddle desperately with braces, suspenders, buttoned boots, corsets and other appurtenances of Victorian dress. In a frenzy the Viceroy tears at her clothes; at first she tries to resist him, then he remembers the terms of their arrangement and knows there is no hurry, so is calmer and more careful. 'Charles,' she might say softly. Charles was the family name; both generals had been called Charles as well and Bligh imagines them throwing off wigs, scarlet tunics, white buckskin breeches, unbuckling their swords and kicking off their boots beside other beds on their return from the wars. Bob's dead older brother had been called Charles.

Bligh turns away from the window. Such men were on top of life and living, alive at each moment, part of the great force that makes the world and its history. They had fought and governed, 'bitter and violent men', absurd at moments yet not frightened to be absurd, confident of their own place in their own time, splendid and beautiful in the portraits they had left for their descendants. 'Artistic appreciation is not everything,' Geoffrey Kirk had once said when the two of them had been discussing someone and Bligh had commented on this person's lack of visual sense – and this quiet comment on his effeteness often came back to him. He had admired Geoffrey, perhaps almost loved him, and realised that the criticism was just. He knew he should visit Mary but could not face entering that Hampstead house again, to have to discuss Geoffrey with a querulous old woman.

The voices return: Geoffrey, Bligh's idea of the men who made this house. He looks through the window. The Layburns were fortunate to have had money at times of good architectural style and taste. A Victorian architect, it is true, had intruded, yet here again luck had come with the death of the Viceroy and the decision of his heir to call a halt to 'the improvements'. The family then made no further changes, leaving Cragham to rest brilliantly in the chill grey of its surroundings. The house, the garden, the park, the moorland to the north-west of the property; then the few remaining collieries, the small towns joining one another in a rash across the countryside, the now largely abandoned harbour from which the coal and iron ore had once been shipped, and the great towers of the power station on an outcrop of land near the sea. Once past the gates of the drive to the house, the industrial landscape is hidden, yet it excites Bligh. This seems such an apt illustration of what these places should stand for: the rest they should bring, the chance to recover from the world, the ease in which to think, to choose and the confidence born of this ease.

Then there is Bob. He first met Bob some forty years ago in the war when they were in the same regiment. Since then Bligh has had to rely generally on indirect signals, signs of impatience, smiles of presumed pleasure or a few quick sentences, to form his ideas of his old friend. Only occasionally have there been more words, an outbreak of strange eloquence, the unexpected full use of the low voice which seems to deepen any expression of feeling; these moments he will never forget and they have drawn Bob and him closer, or so Bligh thinks. And Bob has not changed; his silences are still strong, with a strength beyond words or wit. He still likes to play the odd trick, to disturb, even to hurt.

Why, for instance, had Bob gone straight to Friedrich to arrange for some work to be done on the Cragham pictures without using Bligh as the contact with the Institute, as he had always done in the past? Bligh knew that if he raised this Bob would look surprised, most probably murmur that he had not wanted to intrude when he imagined Bligh must want to work on his book in retirement: that book on Venetian painting, still unfinished after thirty years. Of course he would not mention the time the work seemed to be taking – but this would be implied perhaps in a glance, a turn of the mouth, a brief sweep of the hand. Bob has not used his mind but it is still there for these games he enjoys. How much does he know? Sometimes Bligh thinks everything and at other times he reassures himself with the thought of Catherine describing her husband's omniscient air as a pose.

Bligh watches Bob and is pleased, really, to see that he and the effect he has on others is still the same. This boy, for instance, this George Loftus: how quickly Bob has established an authority over him, not that this is difficult to do, given the boy's small stature and apparent timidity. Bligh feels sorry for young Loftus. The house is overpowering when you come to it for the first time: the house and Bob together.

So Bob is the same, in his early seventies, a year younger than Bligh: still quietly energetic, still fastidious in the neatness of his clothes, no matter how old they may be. This morning he would be up early to visit a plantation to look for evidence of badgers. Yesterday it was a family of foxes in another wood; the day before there had been some drama involving a colony of bats. Then he has his trees and his garden where he still works, pruning, planting and weeding, returning to his desk in the gun room off the hall where he seems to spend most of his time now, only using the drawing room when he has guests. The natural world seems to give him something that people cannot: some wordless sense of freedom or mystery. From two black labradors he receives the tribute of loyalty and obedience.

On the whole, then, Bob Layburn does not say much beyond a grumble about the weather or a complaint about roe-deer damage to trees. He might ask briefly about Bligh's life at the beginning of his visit; then not refer to the subject again. Here Bligh thinks he can see the way the house has set Bob apart, has given him an absolute self-possession and selfishness within walls that keep most of the rest of the world at bay. Bligh smiles. Of course it is monstrous. And the man is a monster, really.

So why does Bligh come here, once, sometimes twice, a year? The place grows more uncomfortable each time; the draughts are worse, the hot water system less reliable, the dogs less clean. He tells himself it is this air of shabbiness that makes Cragham so wonderfully English: the casual treatment of great possessions, the living naturally with them, that has often been remarked upon by foreign visitors to this country. This is how it seems to Bligh when he thinks about the house while sitting in his South Kensington flat where the comfort can seem almost stifling. Then he looks back with romantic longing to large, badly lit rooms, the family pictures he has come to know so well, the mementoes of the generals and the Viceroy: also the piles of old newspapers and sporting magazines in the gun room, the dog–chewed edges of the carpets, the intensity of the night-time silences broken only by wind or the rain against the windows, the fresh clean air, the smell of burnt ashes, the hiss of the still damp logs as Bob piles up the fire in the drawing-room grate.

Then, he supposes, there is Bob himself: his elegance and his mystery. Bob's walk, for instance: that unhurried stroll, the rhythm of which seems to have stayed unchanged for over forty years since they had first met in the war, Bligh certain that he would not survive, but Bob apparently more interested in joining his friend Henry Aitken to get in a spot of partridge shooting near Cairo. Henry Aitken, another tall man but much louder, was killed at Alamein. A few days later Bligh saw Bob standing alone on the outskirts of the camp. Grief seemed to surround him, keeping the rest of the men away like a roll of barbed wire. Bligh had approached, then murmured, 'About Henry, Bob. I'm so sorry . . .' The face had turned: sullen and implacable. It was no use. This wound needed time, not words which would only tarnish the glow of memory, rattle harshly through the void.

They could not be friends, he had thought then. He had heard of the Layburn family and of their history, of the two generals and the Viceroy. Bob was the first person of this kind he had met, for Bligh's childhood and early youth had been spent in Salisbury where his father was an architect attached to the Cathedral; these had been quiet years, at a small public school, then university and a place at the Harman Institute where he had just started when war was declared. Surely, Bligh had thought, Bob Layburn must have a circle from which he would be excluded, formed in the traditional way of that class at Eton or Oxford: people like Henry Aitken. He could imagine them, large figures in shirt sleeves shouting to one another after the slaughter of small birds, retelling old stories of some incident of the cloisters, some trick played on an ancient schoolmaster or a display of college high jinks. These people had a stronger claim on Bob, Bligh knew – or thought he knew in those days – and he began to dislike the gentle creature who was happy at other times to identify the North African birds by their calls, to describe with unfeigned delight the sight of a fox glimpsed in the headlights of a jeep. Bob told Bligh he was making a checklist of all the birds he saw during the war. Often Bligh had seen either in a tent or barracks the pieces of loose paper clipped together, covered with the correct ornithological terms.

Once they were in a desert encampment, walking together around the perimeter, checking the sentries. It was dark, a deep blackness, and only the dim light of the few lamps at various points guided them on their round. They were speaking of what they missed, the part of peacetime life they looked back to with the greatest longing. Bligh said something about music, mentioning a concert by Rubinstein at the Wigmore Hall just before the outbreak of war; then waited, expecting an awkward response. Instead there had come a few words so apparently full of meaning and sorrow: words about home, how Bob wished to be back there, how he knew every inch of those woods and longed for the tracks and paths he and his brother had known as boys. 'But Charles was killed at Dunkirk,' he said. 'A direct hit on his boat. They never found him. So now I'll be on my own.'

As the words vanished, as the speech came to an end, the two of them chanced to pass a lamp, to emerge out of the darkness for an instant before it closed in again; and Bligh had turned briefly towards Bob to see his sad yet oddly ecstatic face. Bligh had thought then of the future this man might have: either made crude by the world and time, by the company of people like those other young officers with whom he shot partridges, sand grouse and pigeons, or rubbed out by death. Bligh remembered the photographs of those young men killed in the First World War in memoirs written by the survivors. Bob was like them. He too seemed to speak of a timeless grace, an undisturbed innocence, an immortal past: myth brought suddenly to life by the light of a lamp and recollected joy.

So they had grown closer. The mystery of this quiet, shy man began to possess Bligh, for he knew that Bob Layburn had this other side, another feature perhaps of his background, again a reminder of the sacrifice of that generation in the trenches: the brightness of courage in the face of death. He rescued a soldier from a burning tank, then was decorated again for rallying his men in the face of a sudden attack. Bligh had not witnessed these incidents and Bob had spoken about them only briefly – to say that any officer would have done the same. No, this was not true. Bligh thought of his own panic whenever the shooting started, of how he had to exercise a terrified self-control to stay in his place and disguise his feelings from the others. He had no courage. Bob Layburn was a hero in the tradition of his military ancestors, those men from whom Bligh cannot separate him even now, whose shadows inspire deference still in spite of his attempts to think of them stripped of the dignity of their portraits and reputations, as careerists who chased after honours and whores.

Bligh had believed that Bob must be killed because of this recklessness and he waited for the news of his death. But they had both survived. Bob thought of staying on in the peacetime army and the army would in some ways have been a good career for him with his liking for action and adventure, his gift of command. He decided instead to learn about farming and forestry, then his father died and he had come to live here. And he had married, with Bligh as his best man. Yes, Bob had married Catherine.

Bligh turns away from the window. The room is cold, in spite of the one-bar electric fire he has turned on. He knows the truth beneath these thoughts. He comes to Cragham because of her, because he wants to rake over and over again some of the talks they used to have, their words an extraordinary contrast to Bob's silence: those long out-pourings of words. He thinks of her in this house with the two boys, her children: of the sound of her calling to them, their footsteps on the staircase, the way she would throw open the door of the hall to let them rush into the garden.

What is left? The house, Bob himself and the boys: one a soldier, the other in India. And the cold which seems to preserve these memories like bodies in ice.

Bligh is standing at the sideboard when George comes into the dining room.

The old man is dressed in a long white towelling dressing-gown which covers a pair of pale blue pyjamas: his pose a little absurd as he turns, the lid of one of the dishes on the hotplate held in his hand like a miniature shield, to look over the top of his tortoiseshell-rimmed spectacles. His sparse grey hair is arranged in thin strands over the crown of his head and he gives off a slight smell of violets.

'Good morning,' he says, elongating the first syllable of

the second word. 'I trust you slept well.' Then he helps himself from the dish and walks slowly, carrying his plate in one hand and a large cup of coffee in the other, towards the oblong table at which three places have been laid, and sinks into one of the dark leather chairs. He removes his spectacles, folds them hurriedly with a sharp click, puts them into the breast pocket of his dressing-gown and begins to eat, chewing noisily, his eyes glazed in a trance of pleasure, his cheeks bulbous at first, then slowly deflating as the food leaves them. Recovering his breath he speaks once more. 'Our host has been up early, investigating the habits of a group of badgers.'

'Oh?'

Bligh laughs. 'Yesterday it was foxes. Even at his age, the excitement of these nocturnal watches has not palled. Rather admirable, don't you think? Are you interested in that sort of thing? Bob has tried to teach me a little but none of it stays up here for more than a few minutes.' He taps the side of his head with a thin finger. 'Now tell me something. You mentioned last night that you lived in Mrs Kirk's house. I used to go there sometimes in Geoffrey's day. Is the Vandermeulen still in the drawing room, and that collection of architectural drawings? He had a good eye.' Bligh laughs, screwing his face up towards his eyes, giving himself an oriental look. 'I expect Mary has changed nothing. What does she think of Herbert?'

'Herbert?'

'Friedrich. Geoffrey's successor. She would most probably be too kind to say. Or perhaps not – for Mary could be forthright if the occasion demanded it. I must ...' He looks at his plate and then at George. 'Is she happy?'

'I think she misses the Professor.'

'Ah yes.' Bligh pauses again. 'You know, the two men demonstrate rather well the changes that have taken place at the Institute: Geoffrey always neat in a grey suit, a man of modest demeanour; Herbert Friedrich running around with his tousled hair and great bow tie flopping everywhere, gesticulating while he speaks of some new theory. Yet Friedrich is a passionless man. Wouldn't you agree?'

The door opens and Beryl looks in, wearing a pale blue overall.

'Everything all right?'

Bligh smiles graciously. 'Yes, thank you so very much.'

'I'll clear away later then.'

'Thank you so much.'

The door shuts behind her. 'Oh dear, I think she wants us out of here,' Bligh says. 'But it seems a pity to hurry. In any case I imagine you can't start work until Bob appears. Are you warm enough? Would you like the other bar of the electric fire?'

'No thank you. I'm quite comfortable.' He looks at the great high ceiling, where all the heat must be, then out towards the windows and garden. 'How beautiful.'

Bligh laughs and raises his hand. 'Yes. Catherine loved this room.'

'Catherine? I'm sorry . . .'

'Bob's wife. She died.' He smiles.

'Did they have children?'

Bligh raises his coffee cup to his lips and takes a gulp. 'Oh yes. Two boys.' He stretches his short arms and raises them above his head. 'Charles, the older one, is in the army. He must be almost forty now.' Bligh looks away from George. 'Catherine used to worry that he showed no sign of wanting to marry. Not that there was anything wrong in that direction! Plenty of girlfriends, or so I gathered. I told her that the young have so much freedom these days.'

'And the other son?'

'Damian? Oh no one ever sees him. He leads a nomadic existence, mostly in the east: India, Nepal, Thailand, Indonesia, that part of the world. I've no idea what he lives off. Probably the residue of some family trust.' Bligh laughs. 'He did well at school, went on to Cambridge. Then something happened. It was the sixties. A great many young people went astray in the sixties.' He stops for a moment. 'I wonder if he'll give you the portrait to work on. The one of Catherine, done by Burton a year or so after Bob and she married.'

The door opens. This time it is Layburn, dressed in a tweed jacket and a pair of dark brown corduroy trousers. 'I hope you're being properly looked after.'

'We were speaking of the portrait ...' Bligh begins.

'What portrait?' Layburn walks slowly to his place at the head of the table.

'Catherine's.'

'Oh that. It's got a hole in the bottom right-hand corner. Someone must have put his foot through it. Here!' Two black creatures rush into the room: then hear the edge to their master's voice and slink to their places on either side of his chair. 'I'll show the thing to you.'

'Were you up early?' Bligh asks.

'I didn't go.'

'Where is Charles at the moment? We were wondering ...'

'Catterick Camp. Near enough to come home for the odd weekend.' Layburn turns to George. 'Have you met my eldest son?'

'I'm afraid not.'

'He'll be here tonight.'

'I'm so glad you're going to show Mr Loftus the portrait,' Bligh says.

'Oh?' Layburn raises his head to look down on them both. 'But of course.'

After breakfast, George goes to his room to fetch a notebook because Friedrich, the Director of the Institute, has insisted upon a written report on each stage of the work.

The bedroom is cold as he searches through the clothes in

his still partly unpacked suitcase for the small black-covered book he uses for notes or quick sketches of scenes that catch his eye. The sketches are simple, usually a poor reflection of what has moved him, so much so that he once confessed to Mrs Kirk his disappointment at the way experiences could rarely be accurately recorded or remembered. Mrs Kirk prefers to live in the past, to recall perhaps some long-ago trip with her husband to Florence or a summer afternoon in the cloisters of a Romanesque church in Languedoc, how the light had fallen and what Geoffrey had said. Occasionally so complete is the scene she describes, so clear her memory, that he shows he is moved, also oddly frustrated because these experiences seem so perfect. Then she laughs at his solemn expression. 'You look as if you are about to burst into tears, George! Don't worry. When you're my age, you have just as much to look back on – and probably more.'

He knows that Philip Bligh is a man of the past as well: a follower and admirer of Geoffrey Kirk. George remembers once reading an article by Bligh on Palma Il Vecchio in a back number of the *Burlington Magazine* and has heard him mentioned occasionally at the Institute by some of the older staff, particularly the librarian Edith Parr, who seems to have been there forever, almost since the founding of the place by the trustees of Sir Alfred Harman's will.

'He was a dear, Philip. An absolute dear,' Edith Parr said. 'Is that why you want that volume of the *Burlington*, for his piece on the Venetians? I thought so.' She prides herself on her memory. 'He worked with Berenson, you know, as a young man.' George remembers the elegance of the writing, the fastidious use of mandarin English so different to the leaden phrases of most contemporary scholars: also the feeling that the aestheticism was too pronounced, that the shape of the essay mattered too much to its writer: again the sense of an age when physical beauty had been more important to those who wrote about art.

How crude Pat seems beside this. He tells himself that this

is good: a sign of earthiness, of common sense and humour putting the rest of the world in its place. This house, for instance: what would Pat think? He imagines her with him at the window of the bedroom, staring out over the park towards the woods, her red hair close to his cheek. 'There seems to be nothing for miles,' she might say. 'What do they do in this place?' She would look back into the room, at the mess of the unmade bed, while he explained how the industry and mines of the area around had been hidden by belts of trees or the fold of the artificial landscape. There had been coal and iron ore workings here since before the industrial revolution but one man's notion of the beautiful had kept them at bay.

One man? Yes: the architect of the landscaped park. Pat would look out of the window, perhaps smile politely: then start to talk about her friend Brian. At first George believed that Brian must be a relation of hers because he is often linked to stories of Pat's family, of her parents or the aunt with the bad hip. Then Pat said that he was the son of the owner of the house in Kilburn where she had stayed for six months or so at the start of her time in London. Pat does not wholly approve of Brian yet she clearly admires him for when she speaks of his stories of football riots at Stamford Bridge, of the new motorcycle on which he arrived at the door of her building in Swiss Cottage or the way he throws his weight about in the Tandoori takeaway her voice drops in awe.

Like George's father and mother, Pat talks often about the characters of television serials. She and Brian watch these together, he thinks, either in the evening or at weekends when she makes use of her video recorder. The programmes, however, are different to the ones he would expect to see in his own home: harsher, contemporary, usually American sagas of the super-rich. Is this what Pat wants to be? Brian brings her closer to the ruthlessness of these people, if not to their way of life. Once George asked her, 'Did you see the programmes about Byron that were on a couple of years ago?' Byron? The girl had frowned. She knew about Byron, remembered something she had learned at school, but she had not watched the series, had not sighed in unison with women of an earlier generation.

'I can't stop, George.'

These were her words the last time they met, on the day before he was to drive north. He had wanted to tell her more about where he was going, perhaps speak of his excitement at the thought of this great house, but she was in too much of a hurry, rushing towards the front door of the Institute, her hair swaying from side to side. As always it seemed to be the words, or the need for words, that separated them; this makes him think they can share nothing except this itching desire. But no: he strikes his head with one hand. He likes her voice, her way of speaking, her gift of natural expression and (of course) her simplicity.

CHAPTER FIVE

LAYBURN IS WAITING IN THE HALL, THE DOGS BESIDE him.

'Have you seen those?' he asks, pointing at one of the carved creatures crouched beneath the long dark wooden beams of the roof as if they are holding the structure in place. George looks upwards and finds his eyes on the over-developed private parts of a male unicorn. 'It's all Victorian: additions made to emphasise the mediaeval connections. Do you think I should paint them? It would relieve the monotony. Do you see the lighter shade of the panelling compared to the drawing room? If I painted the beasts pale grey, what about that? Or perhaps in two tones – one for the hind quarters, flanks, neck and head: another lighter one for the belly and underneath.'

There are four beasts, as Layburn calls them, two in each half of the room, facing each other across the open expanse. All are clearly masculine: two unicorns and two griffins, crosses between lions and eagles with small compact wings and tongues bared in aggression: the unicorns apparently passive and more gentle with mouths open to show long blunt teeth.

'What does Mr Bligh think?' George asks.

'Mr Bligh?' Layburn laughs, raises his head slightly and again shows the brilliance of his pale blue eyes. How elegant he is this morning in the brown tweed of his jacket, the dark blue tie against the thick, white shirt with black stripes and the grey, hand-knitted pullover: then the thin, tanned, lined face and shock of thick grey hair. 'Oh, it was Philip's idea. He likes to look up at them.' Those clear eyes lock into George's and seem to demand a smile of complicity. 'From here, of course, you have a clear view of the underside. Of the belly.' Layburn lingers on the last word, as if to dwell on its ugliness. 'What do you think?'

'Is it worth drawing attention to them?'

'Oh, I see.' Layburn draws his lips further into his mouth, his face narrowing to a point, like an axe.

George goes on. 'I mean they are interesting, as Victorian additions. But they seem to me to be more a part of the hall's decoration than important in themselves.'

'No doubt Philip will speak to you about it. He has all sorts of ideas for this house.' One of the dogs whimpers, presumably from excitement. 'In the days when we were open to the public, his schemes were most helpful. My wife Catherine and he used to work on it together. Then she died and I turned the rest of the Victorian wing into flats to raise income from another source. I didn't want to have to cope with the opening on my own, so we've been closed for about ten years now. The flats are a help. But I couldn't open the house and have them as well. Come in here.'

Followed by the dogs, they walk together into a small room with walls painted dark green, the same panelling as the hall up to the level of the dado, and a large wooden desk placed so that whoever sits at it can see out to the gravel forecourt. Three or four piles of magazines and newspapers are on the floor, beside the desk. Behind, on the wall, between coloured prints of hunting scenes, is a stuffed fish in a glass case, its eye a sharp gleam caught by the sun. On the frame of the case an inscription reads, 'C.M.L. The Sprey. July 1910. 43 lbs'. A low bookcase takes up much of the wall opposite the window and on top of this lie a double-barrelled shot gun, some boxes of cartridges, a set of binoculars, a pair of secateurs, a selection of seed and plant catalogues, a pile of communications from the Wine Society, a ball of twine and a brown china bowl holding a great jumble of keys.

George looks briefly at the books. The lower shelf holds what appears to be a series of maroon, leather-bound albums with dates stamped in gold on their spines: 1950, 1951, 1952 and so on. Alongside these are some illustrated volumes still in bright dust jackets, mostly to do with flowers or plants or gardens: then on the upper shelf other more technical works about trees and shrubs. A last obvious feature is the tall, glass-fronted cabinet to one side of the window in which stand four more guns wedged securely into their places, barrels pointing upwards.

This room is the centre of Major Layburn's life. It is also extremely cold, with unlit logs in the grate and an electric heater in front of the fireplace on the dark blue and red patterned rug beside two armchairs covered in torn material. The chairs are on either side of the chimney piece with a sofa between them, opposite the fireplace.

'I need the list of pictures.' Layburn searches through two wire baskets which are beside two small leather frames on his desk. The dogs stay quiet at his heels. 'Yes. Here we are.' He brandishes a piece of paper and knocks over one of the frames to show that it holds a photograph of two young children sitting on a wooden seat in a garden. Quickly he stands the frame up again and speaks. 'I thought you would work better in the old library where there's no chance of you being disturbed. It's on the first floor.'

So they go up the stairs and turn left into a large room, where there are books in white cases built into the walls, the leather and vellum of their bindings often cracked and scarred by age or neglect. The air is cool yet stale, as if the windows are rarely opened. There is not much furniture: an old sofa near the fireplace, some hair bursting from one of its arms; a polished wooden chair beside the sofa, another electric heater and a large table with a pile of yet more books.

'Is this all right for you?' Layburn asks. One of the dogs wags its tail. 'Would you like the heater on?' He bends down to a plug by the fireplace, flicks a switch and the two bars of the heater begin to turn red, giving off a slight odour of burning dust. 'You'd better fetch your equipment. I'm sorry I can't help.' Layburn taps his left shoulder. 'Arthritis.'

It takes three trips down to the van to bring up the cases of cleaning materials, the tools of the restorer's trade, the portable easel, the pots of varnish and the sprays. All the time the old man stands watching, a benign look on his face, turning his head occasionally towards the window and the sky from which the sun has disappeared. When the journeys are over and the equipment all on the floor beside the table, he says, 'Over here,' and walks towards four pictures in gilt frames stacked against the bookcase. 'Could you give me a hand?'

Now the room seems warmer and soon the two of them, Layburn panting slightly, have propped the four pictures against the sofa so that they face out into the room. First there is a religious scene: possibly (George thinks) a study of St John the Baptist in the wilderness, lifeless and grimy, by a follower of Correggio. Then comes a romantic landscape, a man on a horse against a dim background of a wooded valley and a rich sky, by a member of the Dutch Italianate school; next an eighteenth-century study of two English foxhounds; and last a modern portrait, again in the romantic style, of a woman from the waist upwards, dressed in black, and apparently floating in front of a large castellated house.

'What do you think?'

The John the Baptist can be brought back to life. There is a chance that after some of the grime has been cleared a lost masterpiece might be revealed: well, not a masterpiece but an important picture which has long lain hidden in the darkness of this unexplored palace. Why not? He merely nods to Layburn, smiles nervously and murmurs something about his interest in these four works that cover a timespan of some six hundred years. The Dutch landscape and the foxhounds interest him less at first, although he wonders if the hounds might be a study for *The Cragham Hunt*. Last of all, he looks at the portrait. How odd. He feels often that he should have more understanding of contemporary work but even this, which is traditional in style, looks crude beside the other canvasses. The woman's skin, for instance: it seems to be of a strange sallow complexion, as if she has covered her face in soft white chalk. Perhaps this has been exaggerated in contrast to her black hair and dark clothes: yet how theatrical. Why could the artist not have resisted the desire to dramatise, to make a statement, in this case a histrionic attempt at romantic melancholy: an attempt which takes both sitter and portrait close to the absurd?

'What do you think?'

Her eyes, large and dark brown in colour, gaze without expression. He searches for something to praise. Perhaps the best touch is the view of the house at twilight across the darkened sward of the park, the thin branches of the trees spread out like the tendrils of a rare sea creature. Then he sees that the house in the background is Cragham and that there is a small thin gash on the lower left corner of the canvas.

'Do you know the provenance of the Italian picture?'

'Provenance?' Layburn frowns.

'How it came to the house.'

'It's been here for as long as I can remember.' Layburn stares at the youth. 'I've never bought any pictures, if that's what you mean.'

'No no no. Of course not. But it looks to me like a good copy of an old master, perhaps in the style of Correggio. I'll have to do research in the Institute's library. On the other hand it might be something even more exciting, by a pupil – or even the artist himself.'

'I see. And the others?'

'The Dutch landscape is a good example of its type, I should think, although again I'll need to examine it more closely. As for the two hounds, perhaps I could have another look at the big picture downstairs. They may be a study or sketch for it. The portrait is a modern work, surely?'

'The portrait? Oh, that's my wife.' He points to the gash. 'Somebody must have put his foot through it. A chap called Burton came up from London to paint her. Oscar Burton. He was in the house for ten days or so. You've heard of him, I expect. His widow wrote to me recently, to say that there's going to be an exhibition of his work in some gallery and they want to borrow this. I told her I don't mind but there's the business of the tear. Then I thought: why not get it fixed now and then the picture will be sound again? And I remembered your people, from a long time ago when Philip used to work there.' Layburn stops. But there is more to come. 'This time, though, I didn't use him. I thought I'd do it myself because I have the address. So I wrote to the head man. Then I told my son Charles and he said: look, if you're going to get someone to come all this way, why not ask him to look at the other things as well?' Again he stops, then starts. 'It used to hang in the dining room. We bought a special frame for it, on Burton's advice. An interesting man. He took us to his studio in London, somewhere near the Fulham Road. Do you know his story? Tragic, absolutely tragic. Suffered from depression – up one moment, down the next. He's dead now, of course.'

'Why did you choose him?'

'Choose him?'

'To paint your wife.'

'He was a name.' Layburn looks at his watch. 'I've arranged for Beryl to bring you your lunch up here. Then you can work right through. Have you got everything you need? Good.' Then the face which had seemed to be cast in marble relaxes into a smile and the voice lowers to a lyrical softness, to hint at great reserves of sympathy. 'But I must show you something that might amuse you, if you feel in need of a rest from the pictures.' He walks to the bookcase that covers the whole of the wall opposite the fireplace, bends down to the lowest shelf and pulls out a large volume bound in dark green leather. 'I'll come to the sofa and we can look it up together. No, please!' Layburn shakes his head, refusing help, and carries the book across the room on his own, his face showing no sign of strain. 'You must keep your strength for your work. Sit here. Do you see the cover?' A gold coronet has been stamped on the leather. 'The Viceroy's symbol. They kept these albums while they were in India. Here he is with some of his staff outside the Viceregal Lodge at Simla. Do you know the place had forty gardeners? Ten men were employed simply to scare off the monkeys. Look at the house! Why did they have to make those places so grim? Philip tells me that the style is known as English Renaissance. Look here at the tennis party, with the usual collection of subalterns and ADCs doing their duty with the women. To be able to flirt properly was an important quality of leadership for young officers in those days.'

Layburn laughs and turns another page to show a woman in a long dark dress and hair pinned up above her neck, sitting at a desk in a room with flowered wallpaper and draped curtains. His hands are brown from work in the open air, strong, yet finely shaped, the thumbs supple and expressive. 'My great aunt in the Viceregal boudoir. What a life it must have been. Do you think she was happy or bored stiff?' Layburn smiles and continues to turn the pages. 'I suppose those enormous rooms were built to impress the natives. Here are the servants. How many do you think there are in that group? A hundred? Two hundred? Even the picnic parties look formal, don't they? Do you think we would have enjoyed it?' His eyes are gentle, slightly dulled, as he looks at George, his brow arched to show he expects a response.

'Can you remember them?'

'Remember them?' Layburn seems put out for an instant. 'What do you mean?'

'The Viceroy and his wife.'

'Oh no. He died in 1892 and she followed a year or two later. I'm not quite as old as that, you know. My grandfather, his heir, was fifteen years younger than he was. There were two girls in between, my other great aunts. My grandfather never cared for his brother and sister-in-law, or Their Excellencies as they came to be called in the family. In fact he wanted to tear down the Mogul room but was prevented from doing so by my grandmother, who thought it should be preserved as an historical curiosity.' Layburn closes the album carefully and stares out towards the chimney piece and the electric fire. 'The two brothers were so different: the one cautious and hard working, known to the civil servants in India as the Tortoise because of his method of slowly covering page after page of memoranda and assimilating volumes of reports and statistics: the other a man of great charm but a gambler, incapable of sustained concentration. It was there our trouble came, with the gambling. My grandfather was foolish enough to imagine he could play the market. Then he lost interest here after two of his sons were killed on the Somme, in the same week. My father had to cut back drastically after the old boy died. Now I do my best, on my own.' Layburn turns to the young man, his smile dying in a look of infinite melancholy.

'But the house is still here,' George says.

'Oh yes. The house is still here.' Layburn tries to stand up, sinks back for a moment, looks suddenly tired, then tries again and succeeds. The pale brown cheek shows signs of red. 'I'm sorry. I've interrupted your work. But I thought you might like to see the books. Are you comfortable? You will say if you want anything, won't you? Well, good luck.' And he leaves, calling to his dogs who have stayed outside in the passage.

Alone, George looks at the pictures with more care.

He sees that he will have to take the portrait and the religious scene back to the Institute: the portrait to be repaired and the other to be worked on over a period of several months when he will try to discover more about it by means of enquiry and research. Then he puts the Dutch picture up on his easel and examines the landscape, seeing gradually how wrong he had been at first. It is soft, with a yearning beauty. Has a stretch of country ever looked so golden, so full of that right light, so close to what he thinks of as the Virgilian ideal?

When young, the artist had travelled briefly in Italy, then returned to Holland never to forget his southern journey. The colours and the tones are true, as he remembers from his own Italian tour one summer while he was still at university, with a friend called Keith Bartholomew. Keith and he had used trains, buses or lifts from kindly motorists to explore Florence, Siena, Perugia, Assisi, and the smaller hill towns of Tuscany and Umbria. They had walked miles, Keith and he, often sleeping outside (people had said they were mad) under trees or orchards, staring at the stars in the blue-black sky. The Italians had been kind, and it had seemed a country of light and joy. Some two or three centuries ago this Dutchman had been similarly moved. But George had found something else, beneath the delight: a slight sadness that he had had only Keith Bartholomew with whom to share it.

The picture does not need much attention. Varnishing will improve it: not too bright, of course, for he knows the importance of subtlety. At his feet lie the tools of his trade: bottles, small jars, brushes, tubes and a large bowl of water he has fetched from the bathroom along the passage. He works for some time, with care and concentration; then he stands back from the easel and looks around the room: at the row upon row of books which may not have been opened for years, the closed white cupboards on either side of the door, the iron-grey sky through the two windows, the three other pictures propped up against the sofa and turned towards him.

He wonders about the woman. Of course Burton has romanticised her. He has joined darkness with a sort of beauty: the dark green of the park's grass, the dark sky, her black dress, black tousled hair, dark eyes with a slight shade of green, then the pallor of her mournful face with the trees to one side of it. Catherine. She holds her hands crossed in front of her: a mistake on Burton's part, surely, for it introduces too strong an element of pose. Yet he can see why Burton has been praised, why there might be interest in this exhibition which his widow wishes to promote.

It is time to start. Friedrich has told him that he must make notes of everything he does: not only the procedures he adopts when working on these pictures but the thoughts and reasoning behind them as well. He picks up the black bound notebook off the table, opens it and sees it is full to the last page with those quick sketches of his: often only a few pencilled lines, yet a form of record he uses like a diary of impressions and memories. So he needs more paper, any paper, for the words can be copied into another book on his return to London. Already there is a certain amount to record, he thinks, as he glances at the Dutch picture on the easel.

Yes. Now for the paper. He looks round the room. All he needs is a scrap, a blank sheet, and there must be something here, something which will save him a journey downstairs. First he opens the cupboard on the right of the entrance. The doors creak, loose on their hinges; for a moment he fears they may collapse; then he sees that inside there are four shelves of copies of the *Annual Register*, starting with the early years of the last century. With care, he closes the cupboard and moves across to the one on the other side. This time the doors seem more firm. Again there are four shelves and again the *Annual Register*, but the lowest shelf is bare except for a small pile of three or four thin loose-covered exercise books of the kind he remembers from his days at school.

This may be the answer. He removes the one on top of the pile, flicks at the cover to shake off the dust and opens it to see rounded writing covering the whole page. Then he reads the first few lines.

Philip Bligh thinks I might be able to write and that to write will help me understand what has gone wrong. I don't know if this is true but the best way of finding out must be to try so I will use the hour or so in the afternoon when Dr Maltby has said I should rest and Charles is looked after by Beryl as my time to experiment. This is always the low point of my day – particularly in the winter when the house is cold and we have week after week of grey skies and the sun seems to forget us completely. At other times what I keep saying to myself seems to have some effect – that I have no reason to be unhappy because I have a beautiful little boy and live in this wonderful place and am married to a man who will always protect me. But in the afternoons when I sit alone upstairs in the small room off our bedroom which Bob says I can use as my own – at my desk thinking of the letters I might write or else in an armchair with a book or a magazine, these thoughts seem not less true but less encouraging or worth remembering probably because I know they will bring no comfort at this time of day. How I have learnt to dread the moment at the end of lunch when Bob stands up to show that the meal has ended and says he must go perhaps to a county council meeting or talk to the forester or the new man at Ford's farm or some business appointment or at the weekends just to work in the garden! Once I almost said please stay, I must tell you – but nothing came as of course it never will.

'He is an honourable man and that was what I always wanted for you– an honourable man,' my father said at the time of the marriage. He respects Bob's position and war record and above it all is this idea of honour. 'It's so marvellous, darling, because he's such a rock,' my mother said. 'You'll always be able to feel that he's there – dependable, brave and strong.'

That was over a year ago. Charles is five months old, our son, the boy Bob must always have wanted. How funny! When Bob and I were out with the dogs in the woods at the far end of the park on Saturday I wanted to mention this in the hope that he might talk to me properly at last but all he said was something about a scheme of replanting he had for another wood. And on this walk, with the dogs running ahead as usual, I felt my mind wandering towards what Philip Bligh had said at one of our lunches in London about how things must end.

Those were his words, I know, because I always listen carefully to Philip. For instance I noticed last time I saw him that there has been a change in the way he says my name. Previously he hardly ever used it and now he seems to take every chance to say Catherine in a voice that is soft and hushed as if he is talking in church. At Cragham it is even more obvious than in London for here he often asks me to walk with him in the park or sit out in the garden if the weather is fine and I enjoy doing this because he has taught me so much but this change of tone worries me as I do not want to be accused of leading him on. Yet we can talk to each other so well and I have confided in him and he has given me such a clear picture of his friend Juan that I feel I've known the boy for years.

I tell Philip he must try to forget about Juan who stole his money and may have been about to do worse. And in the restaurant Philip agreed, saying you must realise when you have reached a limit, for deep in his heart he had known for a long time that the boy was not only dishonourable but without taste or fine feeling as well. So the theft had shown finally that, to use Philip's words, 'the thing must end'.

I felt the talk with Philip was such a strain for us both because he was telling me things he had probably never told anyone else – or at least not in this particular way. Of course his friends must have known about Juan because the boy seems to have been living in his flat on and off for over a year – and they must have suspected something. But he seems to need to tell me so much more about himself now and I give some of the details of my life in return. So what started as me asking him about books, pictures and music has turned into something much more personal – beginning with that afternoon eight or nine months ago when we sat out in the garden here and I spoke a part of the truth about Bob and myself. Afterwards we went back to the house and I had to go to my room for a moment, dreading that I might meet Bob on the way because it seemed as if I had betrayed him. Then, in the bedroom the shame became too much and I broke down on the bed and cried – only for a minute which was lucky for I dreaded either Bob or Philip wondering if I was all right and coming upstairs to look. How rotten and low I felt then but now it comes much more easily and I can say anything to Philip and we still talk most of the time about books and pictures which is the way I want it to be.

There is a knock at the door. He looks up, quickly puts the book back on the shelf, closes the cupboard and returns to his easel. The knock is repeated.

'Come in!'

It is Beryl, breathing hard as she carries a circular tray on which there is a black coffee-pot, a small white jug of milk and a large cream-coloured cup, slightly chipped on the rim. 'The Major thought you might like some coffee,' she says. 'It's eleven o'clock.'

He looks at the tall slightly stooped figure, her white hair neatly pinned up at the back of her head. Then he glances towards the portrait of Catherine Layburn, at what he sees now as the look of distress on its subject's face. 'Oh, thank you.'

'Shall I put it on the table?'

'The table?' he looks around.

'Beside you.' She places the tray a few feet away from where he works, wincing as she bends down.

'Thank you.'

Beryl smiles, her lined face wrinkling upwards towards her clear-framed spectacles. 'What have they given you?' She looks at the easel. 'That's nice.'

'There are these three as well,' he says quickly, watching her eyes as they move to inspect the pictures propped against the back of the sofa. 'You see the tear at the bottom of the portrait.'

She nods and he thinks that she must be very old. 'I can remember that one being painted.' She talks slowly, turning towards him again with a coy smile. 'She wasn't at her best. It was soon after Damian was born.'

'How long ago was that?'

'Oh, over thirty years now.'

'Did the artist come to stay?'

Beryl frowns, worried lest she mislead this young man. Ever since her childhood in the nearby village, she has set great store by the truth. As a young girl she was once thrashed by her father for lying and has never forgotten this. She knows that most people have thought of her always as slightly simple or 'not quite as others', as she once heard her mother say. But she has (she thinks) what these others do not seem to have: this gift of remembering what people say or do long after they themselves have forgotten. Perhaps it is because her head is empty of things like children, family life, a husband, keeping a home. The gaps are filled with memories.

Now this young man wishes to know about Mr Burton, the painter, probably because they are both in the same line of business. 'He was here just under a week,' she says. 'He came on a Tuesday and took the train back the next Sunday afternoon. It was in the winter – the beginning of December. We had to put paraffin heaters in this room to keep the two of them warm. Yes, whenever there's been any painting to be done, this is the place they've chosen to do it.' Her brow clears. 'We never saw Mr Burton again.'

'What do you think of the picture?'

'Oh, I don't know. As I said, she wasn't at her best. The baby had only been born a couple of months before and she was lovely to look at. But Mr Burton got something of her. I don't quite know how to say it.' She looks back at him. 'She could have that sad look. I don't mean she was always moping about. But I came to know her because I looked after the children in those days – and she could draw away from you, if you see what I mean.'

'I shall have to take the picture back with me. The tear can't be mended here.'

'Where will you take it?' The old woman is still looking at the pale face on the canvas.

'To London. To the place where I work.'

'And they repair pictures there?' Her face now turns towards him. 'It hasn't been hung for a long time. They used to have it in the dining room, over the fireplace. But after she died, it was taken down and then the damage was done in some way, I don't know how. Since then it's been kept up here, face to the wall, propped against the bookcase. Sad really, because no one comes into this room now.'

'Not even to look at the books?'

'The books?' She stares at the shelves. 'Well, they're all

rather old, I should think. They've never been used in any case – not while I've been here. Some visitors have shown an interest, though: that's true. Mr Bligh, for instance. He was keen. I remember him saying to me years ago that we ought to get something done about them before it was too late. But that's the trouble in a place like this: you can't keep up with all the work that needs to be done.' She looks again at the portrait. 'But at least you'll be able to mend the hole.' She turns towards the door. 'Here am I talking away when there's work waiting for me downstairs. Just leave the things on the tray when you're finished. I'll be up just before one o'clock with your lunch. The two gentlemen are having theirs in the dining room but you're to eat up here – or that's what I've been told.' And she leaves the room, the soles of her flat shoes squeaking against the bare boards.

CHAPTER SIX

Bligh SITS IN THE DRAWING ROOM, A NEWSPAPER which he does not read on his lap.

Bob and Catherine. They had been married in London, in a church in Piccadilly, with Bligh as the best man. Then he had hardly known her, apart from a spring weekend at Cragham when she and Bob were about to become engaged. It was a whirlwind courtship, to quote Bob's words.

He had been surprised to be asked to Cragham that weekend, for Bob and he had not seen much of each other since the end of the war. Bligh had returned to the Harman Institute where Ashton, the director in those days, gave him a year's study leave in Italy, first in Florence where he worked briefly with Berenson and then in Venice for a longer period of research. Occasionally, perhaps on a walk in the hills behind Vincigliata or when alone in his lodgings on the Zattere, Bligh had wondered about Bob and had thought of writing, only to dismiss the idea. It must be better not to try to resurrect this strange friendship which had existed only because of the war; after all, Bob and he had little in common. Then, a week after his return to England, the letter had arrived: Bob's neat script, the short sentences. Would he come to stay? He might like to see the pictures. It was sad they had almost lost touch.

There had been four people at Cragham that weekend, in

addition to Bob Layburn and Bligh: a married couple called Tony and Liz Blagden, and Catherine and her sister Sophie. The Blagdens came from Staffordshire where he farmed and bred horses; she was jolly and talkative, he fair-haired and more silent, yet genial as well. Bob had known Tony Blagden since childhood days when the Blagden family had been friends of his parents.

'Did you know old Mr and Mrs Layburn?' Tony Blagden asked Bligh on the first evening as they waited for the others to come down to dinner. 'Super people. Of course they had the most awful struggle here to keep the place together. Then there was the terrible business of Charles, Bob's brother, who was killed at Dunkirk. Did you know Charles? He was one of my greatest friends. You see, we were exact con- temporaries – at school, in the army, right the way through. What fun Charlie was – just like his grandfather, or so people said. We had some good laughs together.' Bligh still remembers the way Tony Blagden had looked amusedly towards the window. 'It might not have worked up here, I suppose. I couldn't see Charlie settling down. But perhaps with a good wife, a child or two. One can't tell. Funny how death suddenly comes into families, isn't it? First old Mrs Layburn, just before the war. Then Charlie. Then his father last year. Like an epidemic, isn't it? Now Bob's got his chance at Cragham. To me he was always Charlie's little brother, running around looking at birds – of the feathered variety, of course!' The laugh was short, discreet. 'But you must know him better than I do. Just fill me in on those two girls. Any chance of wedding bells?'

Bligh thinks back to his first sight of her: a tall girl with her sister, that dark hair, the sweet, slow smile, as if she knew more than her shyness allowed her to say. He had been prepared to despise the sisters, or at least to find them limited and dull; instead their lack of guile, the simplicity of their friendliness, had charmed him. On the Saturday morning Bob suggested a tour of the house and Bligh had found himself talking about the pictures; what had started as a few comments made to his host soon developed into a lecture as the others crowded round. Was it in front of the huge hunting scene or the much smaller Dutch landscape that he had first become aware of her beauty, shown in the earnest look of slight strain on her young face, the result of a determination to learn? He listened to her questions; she spoke hesitantly, the words quiet. Later, with Catherine, he would think often of Lear's tribute to his dead daughter: 'Her voice was ever soft,/Gentle, and low, an excellent thing in woman.'

That weekend the seriousness of the girls seemed to affect Bob, Bligh thought, and draw him away from the Blagdens who were clearly surprised by all this talk about art. Bob too began to speak of the house, to tell stories passed down the family for generations. Once they found themselves alone together in the garden, the Blagdens and the girls having dropped back to look closer at a particular shrub, and Bligh said, feeling he must encourage his friend: 'You're young. Think what you could do here – add to the collection, bring light and life into the house, throw off the dust sheets! Aren't you excited, Bob?' Bob turned to him, smiled and answered gently, 'Yes. But I need help. Will you advise me? Can I come to you from time to time?' In that instant, Bligh had wanted nothing in the world more than this. A month later, Bob's letter arrived to tell of the engagement 'to Catherine who was at Cragham when you came' and to ask him to be the best man at the wedding. Then it seemed to Bligh that the killers of small birds had been defeated, that Bob Layburn had been won for civilisation.

Of course, she was different to the Layburns. At the reception after the wedding, in a big hotel, another guest whom Bob and he knew, perhaps again from the war (he could not recall the name: only a large red face) had joked about the expense and how the Layburn family must be paying because the bride's father's resources extended no further than an officer's disability pension. 'I believe he was wounded in Palestine,' whispered the man and Bligh had said that he hardly knew the girl but she seemed sweet. Then, some six months later, they had met again where he would not have expected to see Bob: at a dinner party in Knightsbridge.

Oh, the chaotic start to that evening! Bligh arrived late, having forced himself to come in spite of the great crisis that had blown up in his life. It had erupted out of a scene with Juan, the Spanish boy with whom he was involved at that time and as usual the row was about money. Juan, a refugee from Franco who had found work in a Bayswater hotel, complained that he could no longer live on his wages and the occasional gift from Bligh. There must be more money or he would leave and the boy hinted that there were offers from richer people; one of the restaurant's patrons was looking for a chauffeur and another had spoken of his need for a bilingual secretary.

It was the word bilingual that made Bligh furious. He knew Juan could not make sense of an English newspaper, let alone complicated matters of commerce. Then, after mentioning the chance of these jobs, the boy had begun to threaten blackmail in ridiculous words that added further to Bligh's rage, for Juan had clearly prepared this with the aid of a dictionary. So Bligh lost his temper and, raging alternately in English and Spanish, tried to remind Juan what he had done for him. He had given him a home, taken him off the streets, picked him out of the gutter . . .

Suddenly, in the midst of his fury, Bligh saw the truth. Juan was a fraud and a crook. The boy was also cruel, with the strength of the ruthless. Yet if he left, Bligh would lie alone night after night, regretting the loss of the strange joy he felt in Juan's company, the sense of treading a path above a dark chasm. His words faded, the fury cooled while Juan waited. Then Bligh went to his room, slammed the door, changed for dinner and left the flat, noticing on his way out that the boy's overcoat was not in the cupboard in the small entrance hall. Juan had gone.

So that winter evening Bligh was upset. Let the imbecile leave, let him see how he manages; or let the little crook do his damnedest, let his bluff be called and the threats revealed for what they were: the impotent ravings of a guttersnipe. As the taxi carried him towards Knightsbridge, these thoughts wheeled like vultures around a corpse. Bligh knew that something was dead which previously quickened the routine beat of his own slow pulse.

He pushed the bell, smiled weakly at the grand figure in black who took his coat. Bligh was used to this sort of occasion. He dined out often in London as a single reliable man. Already the drawing room held some eight or nine people. Melissa, his ageing hostess, advanced, her smile cold, for he was late. To her the whole business of Juan would be unmentionable, yet if she knew she would not condemn Bligh, for Melissa was aware of the world and its tricks.

The introductions were made: an ambassador, a Member of Parliament with good social connections, an American millionaire who kept a flat in London, a fashionable portrait painter: all accompanied by their wives, all known in varying degrees to Bligh who came frequently to the house. He smiled and exchanged kisses; then noticed, slightly apart from the rest of the group, Bob and Catherine Layburn whom he had not seen since their wedding. Bob, awkward, began with the joke, 'You remember my wife?' She raised her eyes from the floor to offer a hand which he rejected in favour of a kiss.

He was next to her at dinner, with the wife of the Member of Parliament on his other side: an acidic woman, thin as a stick, dressed in black with her hair twisted and curled like a nest of serpents, who spoke of a villa she and her husband owned near Antibes. Her words were a cover under which he could imagine the Spanish boy.

'Yes,' he replied. 'How far from Nice? You say you can

fly there any day of the week?' Not to be alone was, he supposed, some sort of comfort.

Then he turned to Catherine. This evening, he thought, there were no surprises: only her beauty, which was undeniable: dark yet with what he thinks of as an English freshness and simplicity, not at all exotic, with no connection to the great Venetian pictures on which he had been lecturing that afternoon. He wished then that he need only watch the girl in silence, for he believed she would have to be coaxed out of herself, a process for which he feared he might not have the energy this evening. Bligh remembered how appreciative she had been that weekend at Cragham before her engagement. She was serious and wished to learn, and he must put Juan out of his mind. How did she and Bob come to be here, he asked, without mentioning his surprise at finding his old friend in a house like this.

Catherine spoke slowly, careful with her words. Bob was a cousin of William's, she replied, and Melissa had heard they were in London briefly, so had asked them round. William? Oh yes, Bligh thought: the invalid husband, a prisoner in a house on the Berkshire Downs. He should have known. Most people of Bob and William's type were related, forming a great network of cousins, nieces, nephews, aunts and uncles that seemed at times to include not only this country, but Europe, the United States, indeed most of the western world. In the war Bob had spoken of relations in Cairo, Calcutta, Rome, even among the Free French in Algiers: not saying if he particularly liked them or not, merely remarking on their ties of blood, occasionally dignifying or condemning one with a short word or phrase – 'great fun', 'drinks too much', 'sent down from Oxford', 'ladies' man', 'can't understand her', 'difficult wife' or 'haven't seen him for years'.

'Have you known William and Melissa for long?' Catherine stumbled slightly over the Christian names, then blushed, raising her head so that he could see the redness on her neck. He answered that he had met Melissa some years ago; William he scarcely knew. What he did not say was that he had cultivated friendship with this woman, had made himself available to act as an escort perhaps to the theatre or a concert or a private view. They used each other; that evening, for instance, he was a spare man to take the place of her absent husband, and in return Melissa was one of his links with society and the world of riches. Suddenly he felt contempt-ible, ugly, fat, balding, cynical, world-weary and weak before the outrageous wrongness of his life.

'How long are you both in London?' he asked.

She smiled as she told him that they were only down for three days and she had to be careful because their first child was expected in six months' time. Then the girl glanced across the table to where Bob was, next to Melissa, and her look seemed to speak of such yearning: of a pure love for Bob himself, the Bob whose elegance and distinction had drawn Bligh to him as well. An image grew in his mind: an image of the two of them at Cragham with children, their feelings contained within the bright circle of themselves and their family, free from guilt or shame, their beauty (for both of them were beautiful) turned towards each other yet obvious and enviable to all who witnessed these two young lives.

'Where are you staying?' he asked.

Catherine's smile faded: a smile that hid her and Bob's mystery, the secret of the way they were together. She named an hotel.

'Sometimes we go to my parents,' she said. Then she smiled again. 'But I think Bob prefers the hotel. He doesn't have to talk at breakfast.'

'I wish Bob had told me you were coming down. I'd have liked to have done something. We could have had dinner together, gone to the theatre or met up with some old friends.' Then he thought: which old friends? He knew nothing of their life now. 'What are you doing tomorrow?'

'We're having dinner with my parents. Bob has to see the lawyer.'

He remembered. 'There's a lunchtime concert at the Harman Institute. I asked Melissa but she can't come because William is in London for the day. I'd be delighted to take you both.'

She looked worried. 'What kind of concert? Bob isn't very musical, I'm afraid.'

'They're doing the Schubert D minor quartet. And the Debussy as well.' He felt excited. 'Why not come alone?'

'I must ask . . .' she began.

'I'm sure Bob won't mind. I'll telephone your hotel in the morning.'

Then they were interrupted. Melissa had spoken of Bligh's time with Berenson and the American wanted to hear about I Tatti, having once known some relations of Mrs Gardner. The Member of Parliament joined in to ask about the Institute's purchasing policy and what Bligh's views were on the need to discourage the export of works of art; the ambassador explained the procedures used by his own country in these matters. Always courteous, Bligh played his part, telling two short anecdotes about Mr Berenson, listening attentively to the politician, commending the ambassador's compatriots for their wisdom, impressed all the while by Bob's silence which seemed to deepen in proportion to the shallowness of the talk. The Layburns left soon after dinner, pleading tiredness, and Melissa remarked, 'A sweet couple. So shy. But I think they enjoyed themselves, don't you?'

The next day Bob was happy to let Catherine go to the concert while he had lunch with the family solicitor. At the Institute Bligh introduced her to Ashton, the director, and to Geoffrey Kirk, then Ashton's deputy, whose idea these midday performances had been. Afterwards he took her to lunch in a nearby French restaurant and here, in front of her calm sympathy which seemed to hold the possiblity of limitless forgiveness, he spoke of himself, the words coming faster as he drunk glass after glass of wine. Truths he had told no one about the crisis with Juan: these must appal her but he saw that he had to speak, that this was the time – in the company of a girl who was almost unknown to him. There seemed no reason for this. Bligh had had several women confidantes in his life, for he found them easier to talk to than men. Was this different? He thought not but now he remembers only her sympathy. She seemed fascinated, even moved: worried for him, yet not shocked. 'I am a criminal,' he almost said. 'Aren't you appalled?'

They had ended by agreeing to write. Soon he would come north: as soon as possible, she hoped, to talk and to help her with the house. After they had parted, he realised that she had told him nothing about herself; then he thought this did not matter because she must be happy and to discuss such a condition was generally pointless and dull, even for those who were able to share it.

CHAPTER SEVEN

In the old library, sunlight pours through the two large windows: the winter sun that is warm behind glass.

The Dutch landscape is on the easel, the Utopian scene of a horseman in the orange and dark green glow of a southern landscape at twilight. George thinks of the picture and this dead woman's writings, and of himself as an intruder. To brighten the Dutchman's work, to remove some of the signs of age: is this not trespassing upon the artist's original vision? Friedrich would think so. Then he would say that this is why rules must be obeyed, rules which lay down the importance of doing as little as possible to a picture when it comes into your hands.

Of course he will be careful. Yet he must come between a work of imagination and the mind of its creator. After he has finished, the picture will be at least partly his, no longer entirely the Dutchman's. Perhaps this is some sort of secret triumph, an act of discreet creation.

Through the window he can see out across the grass to some derelict buildings. Beyond these are the tops of some trees, grey in the sunlight. Where is the wood in which Catherine and Layburn had walked? Perhaps on the other side of the house, at the far end of the park. He looks again at the exercise book.

Bligh still has the newspaper on his knees. Were they lovers, he wonders: Catherine and that man? Were they lovers? Stefan. She is dead. He cannot ask. Such prurience is disgusting and wrong.

I rang Philip yesterday evening but I could get no answer – once the line was engaged and I thought another person must be trying to get hold of him as well, perhaps Juan, and this may be why he is either out or not answering. So I wrote to him instead, saying that I hope he will come here again soon, although I know this place is not very nice in the winter – because a visit would make all the difference to me now when there seem to be so many of these afternoons to get through before the better weather comes and we can spend more time in the garden.

Bob was in one of his moods last night. He asked me if I'd read about the Huddersfield murder in the newspapers and I said no and he said how strange it was that they had seemed such a close family – the husband, wife and three small children in their new house on the outskirts of the town. Hadn't I seen the photograph of the man and his wife on holiday in Harrogate with a group of friends? Bob asked. No, I answered, I'd seen nothing about it at all. Well, he said, they found the body in a wood near the new house and nobody could think of a motive for the killing – with the happy family life, the honest business career and the work the man had done for charities. All this time Bob's clear eyes were on mine and I seemed to feel them burn into my head. No, I almost screamed, turn away – then he said something about the secrecy of some people's lives and how they could live in two worlds, one completely separate from the other and I thought of Philip and told Bob I had asked him up here to help with the rearrangement of the rooms the public see. 'Oh yes?' is the answer, followed by an angry tightening of lips, and I see now that I should have spoken to Bob first before writing the letter, even though they are supposed to be old friends.

Sometimes I hear him laugh with Beryl, in the downstairs passage or when they meet in the hall and they do not know that I am there – and she laughs as well, usually after telling him something which I can't quite hear, most probably about the baby who I know she wants to keep to herself. He must be in league with her – for what other reason does he keep saying to me that I need more rest and Beryl can take charge of Charles? Of course they have known each other since they were children because both her mother and father used to work in the house in the old days. I wonder what they say and what secrets they share and why Beryl never married because she is pretty when she smiles which she often does for Bob. But she seems to have given up her life for us now that she was moved out of her parents' cottage by the South Lodge into the old night nursery on the top floor where she sleeps next to Charles.

This is my world now – walks with the pram round the garden, hoping the baby will not wake in the night, talking about him to Beryl when he cries or seems not to be interested in his food – and the long rests in the afternoons on the doctor's orders. At least I am no longer so tired so I do not go to bed quite so early. But the distances in this house ... Yesterday evening I left the top floor after Charles had been put down for the night. I knew what I had to do – go to the basement, to the kitchen, to prepare the dinner in time for it to be in the dining room by eight o'clock which is when Bob says we must eat. On the stairs I walked past the first floor, then through the hall, along the passage to the pantry, down the three flights of stone steps on to the great flagstones of the kitchen, hearing my footsteps echo through the empty spaces. The kitchen is warmer, for the iron range is filled with coke twice a day by Alfred, the garden boy, and for a moment I stopped, enjoying the warmth after the cold of the stairs and the rest of the house, for the fire in the dining room, lit in the morning by Mrs Webster who comes in from the village, has no wood put on it after half past three which is the time she goes home. Then I remembered that not only must the fire be going again before eight o'clock or the temperature in the dining room will drop to arctic levels but the table should be laid as well, so up the stone steps I went once more, into the pantry across from the dining room, to the long wooden table and the cupboards built in to the walls of the room that hold the plates, glasses, knives and forks. For a moment I thought – surely the fire is for Bob to look after, surely he should lay the kindling on the top of the pile of ashes, fetch the old newspaper, arrange the logs in such a way that their dampness will not make it impossible for the kindling to set them alight. Yet he does not need the fire for he does not feel cold. Oh no. It is for me. Should I say – won't you do it, please?

No. I will not, for at dinner Bob can be awkward. To him the evening meal is an occasion. At home, of course, it was supper, but here we have dinner and I believe he would really like to change into a black tie and only the fact that I am cooking the meal prevents him. As it is, we have to eat in the dining room for this is the way it has always been, in his parents', grandparents' and great-grandparents' day. To have dinner in the kitchen would be unthinkable. He talks sometimes of replacing Beryls' aunt who had been the cook for twenty-five years before her death six months ago, but I know there is no chance of anyone coming for the wages he says we can afford – so we will go on like this.

No one warned me that I should be so much alone.

I have tried to find out more about the history of this place. Bob gave me the pamphlet written by the Viceroy when he was an old man called 'The House and its Contents' and said I ought to bring it up to date and write a proper guide book for the visitors who at the moment are only given the typed sheet of paper done by his mother before the war. 'Philip will help,' he said and I am interested in the pictures and the house, but it is the people I want to know more about – not the ancestors, the generals and the Viceroy because he does speak of them – but Bob himself and his parents who I never met and yesterday evening it seemed as if Bob might be going to tell me at last. We were sitting in the drawing room after dinner and I had begun by talking of the weather and then Charles, who is not sleeping well. He listened, but I felt something was wrong because his eyes stayed on me only for a brief moment at a time. Would he tell me? I stood up, said I would put the dogs out and have a late bath. I called to the dogs. They got to their feet. Then, as I passed the back of his chair, he said, 'He used to hate them getting wet at night.' He? I stopped. I could hear the rain against the windows. The dogs started to paw the carpet and I told them to sit. 'My father always wanted to keep the dogs dry when he put them out last thing,' Bob went on. 'Funny, isn't it? As soon as I was old enough that was one of my tasks – to dry the dogs. At first I was rather frightened. Labradors seem huge to a small boy.'

Bob spoke slowly and if I had had a pencil and pad I could have taken down all he said. I edged back from the door towards the chair opposite him on the other side of the fireplace, praying the dogs would behave and not give him an excuse to stop and thank God they came after me slowly and lay down in front of the fire.

This was not the first time he had spoken to me about his father, or not quite the first. No, when we first met he told me he was now alone for his parents had both died and his older brother Charles had been killed in the war and I have often imagined them all here together during his childhood – with secret games in the garden, the sound of the wind outside the boys' bedroom, the children running down the long passages. I have always wanted to know more and last night I thought – perhaps this time – but all he said was, 'My father had a way with dogs. He liked to breed from them.' Then he stopped, looking at me with those fierce clear eyes. 'I'll be up soon. Are you tired?'

CHAPTER EIGHT

HE IS WORKING ON THE DUTCH LANDSCAPE WHEN there is a knock at the door.

'Come in!'

Beryl walks slowly with the tray.

'It may be a little cold because I had to bring it all the way up here with only a cover to keep the heat in.'

'I'm sure it's fine.'

'So you haven't started on her yet?'

'Her?'

'Mrs Layburn.' She stares at the picture on the easel, still holding the tray. 'I like that one.'

'Please, the tray can go here.' He points to the table. 'I'll fetch a chair.' He looks round, sees the polished wooden chair beside the sofa and brings it across.

'Do you know, that was one of her favourites, that one you're working on now? She once told me she could stand and look at it for hours on end.'

'Tell me, do you miss her?'

'Mrs Layburn? She was very ill, you know. In terrible pain. She wanted to die. The Major said to me afterwards that it was a blessed release. But I try not to remember her as she was at the end – thin as a rail, so thin it hurt her to turn in bed. No, I don't like to think of that.'

'Was she beautiful?'

'Before her illness? Oh yes. Beautiful but quiet. She was a quiet person.'

'Did she do much to the house? Did she make many changes? Your parents were here before you, weren't they?'

She smiles, a slow spread of warmth over her face. 'The Major always did the garden. That was his and nobody was ever allowed to interfere without him knowing exactly what they were going to do. Mrs Layburn did change some of the rooms about. She put new curtains up in the dining room, I remember that.'

'What did she do here?'

'Do?' The old woman looks blank, as if every thought or memory has been wiped from her head.

'How did she keep herself busy?'

The slow smile returns. 'Oh, she made sure the house ran smoothly. And there were the children of course. Have you met Charles and Damian?'

'No.'

'Well, Charles is coming up this evening from Catterick. He's in the army. And Damian – well, we don't hear much from him. He went abroad some years ago. At first I used to get a card every Christmas, regular as clockwork, but they've stopped coming now – probably because he's nowhere near a post office. The Major gets a letter sometimes. He tells me the boy seems happy. It's a pity he's so far away, though.' She pauses, then the smile comes again. 'They're good lads. Now I'd like to see them settled. But there's time enough for that, I dare say.'

I wish I had been better prepared for what was coming to me although before I married Bob my mother had tried to explain what I ought to expect.

We were alone in the sitting room at home and I remember her expression because I had seen that face before – some five or six years earlier when she had discussed my period with me and explained how this was all a part of growing up. Now she did not know if Bob and I had made love together or even if I had been with someone else.

'I'm sure Bob will be careful.' This was as far as she felt she should go. I did not tell her we had only once kissed each other, for to have admitted this would somehow have betrayed the two of us and I wanted that side of things to be marvellous and secret so I gave her no help. 'Are you travelling to Scotland by train for your honeymoon?' she asked. I said that we were. Bob had booked us into a fishing hotel he knew on the Spey where he said the country was beautiful with wonderful places to walk. He might fish a little, depending on the weather and the height of the river. We could not be away for long because he had business to attend to at Cragham and he wanted us to settle there together as soon as possible.

Then my mother did what she usually does when she is not sure of herself – started to talk about something else. This time it was some Scottish trip she and my father had made years ago, to Loch Lomond, soon after they had married but before I was born. She mentioned a picnic in a hidden glen, a walk across a moor in the rain and I wonder now if perhaps the two of them had found each other there in a way they had never done previously, not even on their honeymoon in Cornwall, and for her Scotland means the end of shyness and doubt. Is that why, at the end of her story, she repeated, 'I'm sure Bob will be careful'?

'Careful of what?' I had to say it although I knew she would blush. 'You may know already, dear . . .' she answered. 'You probably do. Things have changed since I was your age. Your father and I, for instance. We never . . .' She stopped, then started again but with those words left out. 'Before we married, that is. And if you are not prepared, it can come as a bit of a surprise, if you see what I mean.' My mother laughed in a strange wild way. 'I'm sure Bob will be careful.' Then suddenly she seemed inspired and the awkwardness disappeared in a way I had seen before when some crisis blew up or my father had a failure with one of his schemes – as if she suddenly felt she could show that strength she kept for emergencies. At last the words came. A woman must remain calm. In marriage there are obligations. I must stop her if she was telling me what I already knew, for she realised that the war had changed ways of behaviour. She would not blame me if Bob and I had pre-empted the marriage ceremony. No, she said, she would not blame or condemn me at all if I was no longer a virgin. But in the Speyside Hotel ... She stopped, short of breath.

I said nothing. Of course I had thought of Bob and this, and when he and I had kissed on the lawn in the dark at that dance in Gloucestershire, I had believed that I had felt something within me – something new, although I had been kissed before by two or three men, each time at a different party, twice in London, once near the tennis court of a house in Barnes. No, this was different, for it seemed the perfect expression of all I hoped for in Bob – the first roughness turning to a tender, sad man whose strength could be gentle and kind.

But in the Speyside Hotel ... My mother began again. Marriage involves certain obligations, she said. I was going to be given a new life, much better than this – and here she raised one hand and waved it over the small sitting room. Her laugh now was calm and I knew she was thinking of Cragham. She and my father had been there at the end of the winter with me, as Bob's guests, soon after we had become engaged. The sun had shone, lighting up the dark house, and it had seemed like a palace – yet not so daunting or grand –

no, everything was soft and warm for those three days. Then we had walked out across the lawn in the mild weather, through the park, into the woods and even the power station had seemed somehow magnificent against the clear sky and sea. Bob had been polite, listening to my father's stories of India. He had asked the right questions and explained about the house in his gentlest way.

My mother seemed now to be saying that something was expected from me in return. In the marriage service, she said, there is mention of this and of course we would soon want to start a family. So in the Speyside Hotel ... Again she paused, then rushed on. Certain demands would be made on me, not so much on me but on my person – no, not my person (that was not quite the right word), on my body – yes. 'You will be sharing a room,' she said. 'Think of it as a time of discovery.' The phrase sounded prepared. Had my father and she spoken about this? Then she added that if things were difficult in Scotland I must remember that Bob and I had years ahead of us – years and years in which to get it right.

She smiled with relief. Her ordeal was over. 'When are you seeing the dressmaker?' she asked. And I remembered I had a fitting that afternoon and should hurry to the shop in Knightsbridge or I would be late.

In those months before our wedding I felt sure I was in love with Bob and this seemed to grow with each meeting. He had to be mostly at Cragham, setting the place in order, as he called it, having finished the course at the agricultural college in Kent – but he tried to come to London as often as possible to stay with his aunt in Bryanston Square. Then he would take me to meet some of his relations. They were friendly but grand, in a quiet way, or most of them were. They knew I was different and slightly to be pitied. One aunt wanted to know how Bob and I had met and I explained that people used to feel sorry for my sister Sophie and me and ask us to the country for weekends in the summer. Then we were living at home, leaving each morning for our secretarial course – so it had been a relief one Friday in June to take the train to Moreton-in-Marsh to visit some of my mother's cousins.

This was the weekend that changed my life. On the Saturday night there was to be a dance given by some neighbours. Gladys and Tommy, our host and hostess, lived in a grey stone house on the edge of a hill with a garden that went down towards an orchard of apple trees. 'Of course, dears, you never did a season, did you?' Gladys said once to us and I knew this was where my mother wanted us to be, that the other guests were the sort of people she wanted for us. She worked hard to build a home with nice polite children and her husband as head of the household. 'Your father says this, your father says that,' – or 'Sophie, no running in the passage, darling, because your father has to work late tonight in his study.' In return she had his love shown in the way he kissed her whenever he returned to the house, the way he limped sadly towards his wife, and I felt these young men staying with Tommy and Gladys near Moreton-in-Marsh were the point of it all, men like the tall, elegant, shy Major Bob Layburn who I met for the first time that summer weekend – not that I needed my mother's wishes then to urge me on, for he alone was enough. On that first evening when Sophie and I, who were sharing a room, came downstairs ready for the dance, everyone else – Gladys, Tommy, the other guests, even Sophie – seemed to be struggling, perhaps to laugh, to find the right words for some story, to draw attention to him or herself and the way he or she could help with the conversation and

I thought then – the tall thin man alone is strong and refuses to be rushed.

At dinner I was beside him and he asked me questions in that wonderful voice. Where did I live? What did I do? He knew Primrose Hill, he said (which I was sure could not be true). There were some nice houses there. Was the secretarial course hard work? Then he talked of himself and how he had left the army to go to an agricultural college in Kent. But there was a complication. Here his voice lowered so far that I had trouble in picking out the words. His father was ill, very ill, in what he described as 'the family house' in the North. His mother had died some ten years ago, leaving the old man on his own. Did I see what he meant? Was it right at this time for him to be mostly in Kent and London – where he stayed with his aunt – rather than back at home?

'The place is in a fearful state,' he murmured. 'I'm trying to learn enough to put it right.' So I asked about his father. Bob leaned back and sighed. The old man had rarely left Cragham at least since the death of his wife. 'When he had his first heart attack, I should have been there,' Bob said. 'I was in Wiltshire with the parents of a friend of mine who was killed in the war.' He stopped talking. I thought men should be like this – secret and beautiful. Yes, there was beauty in the way he looked, in the way his shyness did not affect his elegance. Then he said, 'Would you and your sister visit me in the North?'

That first meeting! I think I must have fallen in love while we were waiting in the hall of the house after dinner to go off to the dance. The other people were laughing and talking and Sophie and I stood on the edge of the group, not knowing any of them well. I saw Bob, also on the outside but nearer the door. We looked at each other. He smiled, an awkward smile as if trying to control it, and seemed for an instant to wink, perhaps (I hoped) passing a signal that from now on we were to be friends. We drove in different cars to the house where the party was – I thought, will I never see this man again? – and I lost him in the crush of the receiving line and the crowded marquee. Someone came up and asked me to dance. I could not refuse, so I danced once – and another person interrupted us and another and another, so I danced with them all, talking as best I could but all the time wondering where he was and knowing it was getting later and later, when suddenly I saw him again, standing beside the entrance to the marquee, still alone. Would he come to me? He held a glass, turned his head as if to take in all the rest of us and I felt a sense of his calm, also a seriousness which seemed for a moment to lift us both out of the crowd. This was what I wanted then – to be grown up, to know more, to speak of sensible and sad things.

The band stopped playing. The dancers started to leave the floor. My partner said something. I turned to him to listen, gave a quick answer, turned back to where Bob had been, saw that he seemed to have left and then heard his voice on my other side. 'May I . . . ?' My partner looked at him. Was he frightened? It was possible because Bob seemed so much older and stronger, more determined in that moment to do what he wanted – and the other man gave me up. The music started once more and before taking me in his arms to go round in time to the new slow tune Bob stood back and said, 'Your dress is wonderful,' putting such meaning into the depth of the words that I forgot they meant the blue and white dress my mother and I had chosen in the spring in a shop off Bond Street for the dances Sophie and I might be asked to in the summer. 'Oh yes,' I sighed. He danced badly but this did not surprise me for to be good at so silly a pastime would not have been right for him and we danced on and on, not talking much as he held me. Later at breakfast with some of the rest of our house party Bob laughed with the others, answered Sophie's questions as I kept looking at him and then we danced again before he walked with me on to the lawn and kissed me before taking me home in his car with Sophie and a man called James in the back. We said goodnight to each other in the passage, saying only what a good party it had been.

Sophie and I were sharing a room.

'Is he wonderful?' she whispered as we lay in bed in the dark and I wondered if she might be jealous. Her dress was a paler blue — just plain blue. As the older of us she had the choice in the shop between the two — the one I wore and hers — but she was too large for the blue and white so had to make do with the more boring pale blue and the style was different — more matronly, as the assistant had said. At first I did not answer so she whispered a little louder in case I had not heard. 'James told me about him. He looks like a hero, doesn't he? You are lucky, Cath. What did you talk about?' This and that, I answered. The music was too loud for us to say much to each other. In any case Bob's father is ill and he did not want to talk.

We went out together two or three times in London, during his father's illness. I felt Bob's misery and almost said as we moved from a restaurant to a nightclub — look, you don't have to do this if you'd rather we just sat together somewhere and were quiet. When he rang me from the North I almost cried to hear his voice.

'I came here last night,' he said. 'He died this morning. The funeral is on Thursday. I have to come down to London next week to see the lawyers. Will you be there?'

Then he came to my home for the first time, to the house in Primrose Hill. My parents seemed to retreat

77

before him, to wait for Bob to do or say whatever he wanted in our small drawing room. My mother's laugh came too easily – I thought, please don't laugh like that because it's not really funny, just embarrassing to hear you, and don't pretend to Bob because I can't bear him to see the lies behind our life. But the army and my father's time in Palestine in the First War saved the evening, for the two men talked about that through supper and moved on to the desert and Alamein and Wavell and Montgomery and Bob's views on all this. Afterwards my father said, 'He told us nothing about himself – nothing about his decorations or his family or the place in the North. Such modesty. How long have you known him, darling?'

Not long. He took me out once more in London, then Sophie and I went to Cragham with Philip and the others, then on another evening in London he asked me to marry him. Then came the first of my mother's talks, interrupted by the appointment with the dressmaker – and the second a week later when she thought she should bring up the subject again. 'In the Speyside Hotel ...' She began with the idea of the place. 'But Bob was in the army, wasn't he?' I'm sure he must have had various experiences that would have ...' Again she stopped, to start again almost immediately. 'I mean, I'm sure he knows.' Then she smiled. The talk, our little private talk as she had called it, was over – or had gone as far as she thought possible. 'Did you want to ask me anything?' she said. Of course I did – in fact I wanted to know it all, all that was hidden, but I said nothing and just shook my head as we both got up from our chairs.

Bob and I had our first night in London, not beside the river Spey.

The plans were made by him. I was told what I should do. If we left our wedding reception too early, it would be thought rude by the guests. If we did not leave the reception early, we would have to take the night train which would be uncomfortable after a tiring and exciting day (I am trying to remember the words he used) so we must stay the night in a London hotel (he would choose a suitable one) and leave for Scotland the next morning.

There were too many people at the wedding. Bob admitted that later and it was his fault because he and his aunt had made a list of guests which included every relation they could think of. Throughout that day, my head reeled. I clutched at incidents to try to steady myself, wanting to draw them out, to make them last long enough for me to be able to see them for what they really ought to be, but this dreamlike feeling was still there, partly because of the fantastic frills and lace and whiteness of the dress itself, the kissing, the sound of the organ in the distance through the open doors of the church in Piccadilly when my father and I left the black hired car to walk together up the aisle, the blur of the faces on either side turned towards us and, at the far end, Bob and Philip turning to look for the bride.

The feeling lasted through the service, the drive to the reception, the long business of shaking hands with the guests, the few words of the best man – then in the car on the way to the hotel in which Bob and I were to spend the night I began to come round. By that time I had changed out of my wedding dress into a smart blue suit, made by the same woman – this and the wedding dress being two things my father had paid for without any help from either Bob or the Layburn family lawyers. As the car pulled away from the pavement – the same large black Daimler that had taken us to the church – Bob turned to me and I saw, for the first time, that look in his eyes – not just the sadness which I had come to know and believe I might be able to help, but suddenly fear. It was there as he spoke.

'I like your suit.' Then a gap before he said, apparently short of breath, 'The day went well.'

He settled back in his seat and stared ahead until the short journey ended and it was time to supervise the unloading of the cases and discover the number of our room. By now I felt alert. As we went up in the lift, escorted by a porter, I knew the time had come and something would be expected of me and when I saw the grand room I thought it right for such a great moment in my life, the true start of our marriage. It was not one room the way I had imagined but a suite of three or four rooms – one large with a double bed, the other even larger with a sofa and chairs, then a small entrance hall (which I thought of as a room) and a bathroom completely surrounded with mirrors so that everywhere you looked you saw reflections of yourself. Bob seemed satisfied and, in front of the porter, clasped my hand, almost immediately letting it go again. The porter stood, not at all embarrassed. Bob turned to him, back to me, then looked at the four suitcases.

'Did the fishing gear turn up?' he asked. The porter, surprised, started to say something but before he had time to answer Bob repeated the question, adding, 'I had it sent straight here because we're leaving for Scotland in the morning and it would only have got in the way at the reception. The wedding reception. We've just got married.'

The porter said he would ask at the desk downstairs, then we went back to silence and Bob gave my hand a short squeeze. Why didn't the porter go? I almost said something, almost asked if he had more work to do when at last Bob reached into his pocket and gave the man the tip for which he had been waiting. The man left. Bob now had his back to me as he lifted one of my suitcases on to the bed and in that moment I had this extraordinary idea of a great tunnel of time ahead of us – all the hours, nights, days, weeks, years of life with a man I hardly knew. It terrified me, so I started to pray which I had not done often since childhood. 'Oh God our help ...' I said to myself, then he spoke and I knew I must listen and answer properly. 'I thought it might be easier ...' he began, then lifted the other case up as well. 'Better get unpacked.' He raised his arms in the air, stretched, then let them fall, looking away from me towards the window through which we could see the grey London evening. His eyes came back to me. Again I saw that strange new look.

'Why don't you take the cupboard and I'll have the chest of drawers?'

So we started to unpack, just a few things, as Bob had suggested. 'I put your cases on the left-hand side of the bed,' he said. 'But don't feel you have to sleep on that side. Personally I don't mind at all. Right or left – it's all the same to me.' And I almost said – oh, so you have shared a bed with someone before, have you? Perhaps he might have laughed. Perhaps that night, that week, that year would have been different because of one remark which could have suddenly brought us together. Instead I went to my side and smiled shyly across at him. 'What a lovely room,' I said.

Already his face had turned away from me to look in one of his open suitcases from which he had pulled out two ties and a white shirt. 'We can ring for more hangers if there aren't enough ...' And as if realising almost immediately the stupidity of this remark when he had not looked into the cupboard, he walked over and opened the doors to show at least ten or eleven hangers on a brass rail. 'Do you want any help?'

I smiled at him and tried to look coy. 'With what?' I asked. By now I too had opened one of the cases and had my hand on a new white nightdress, one of the two my mother and I had bought together for the honeymoon in that shop off Bond Street. I took it out and laid it on top of the pillow.

'Unpacking. Putting things away.'

'No thank you.'

For the train in the morning I had a suit of light brown tweed, made by the same woman who had done the wedding dress and the dark blue suit. This I hung up in the cupboard, brushing accidentally on my way back to my case against Bob who was carrying a shirt to the chest of drawers which faced the end of the bed. Suddenly he dropped the shirt, turned to face me, seized my shoulders and kissed me quickly and roughly on the mouth. So this is it, I thought, and braced myself for something new, so soon. It would be better to get the thing over with, I thought, then heard him say, 'You must be starving.'

Yes, those were the words. He had picked the shirt off the floor and was opening the top drawer in order to put it away. He seemed to be slightly out of breath and I noticed that his hands shook as they pushed frantically at the white material which had now unfolded.

'Bob . . .' I began, then his eyes looked up from where he was, slightly bending down towards the drawer, and I saw the same desperate look and knew that I, even in my ignorant state, must do something to reassure him. So I took the shirt from those trembling hands, held it up to restore the original folds and gently put the thing back into the drawer. 'There,' I said. His look changed to one of astonishment. 'Yes, perhaps we ought to go down to the dining room,' I went on. 'I expect they'll have started to serve dinner . . .'

'No, no. It's all arranged!' He straightened and held up one hand. Then he looked at his watch, the concentration overcoming the fright. The words came fast, probably (I see now) from relief. 'Dinner will be brought to our room at half-past eight. I spoke to the manager yesterday. I told him the circumstances – that we would want to be on our own and go to bed early. He understood.'

There was a knock at the door. 'Come in!' Bob shouted. Two men entered with a trolley. We went through to the suite's sitting room. 'A light supper,' he said quietly, as if to himself, then looked sharply at one of the waiters. 'Bring me a whisky and soda, will you?' The man rushed off, leaving his companion to set up the small table for two. Bob gulped quickly at his drink when it came, before saying to me, 'I'm so sorry. I didn't offer you one. But I've ordered some wine to have with the meal.'

As we sat down together, facing each other across the small table, I felt the silences should end now and I must work harder to bring this about. So when the waiters had opened the wine, served the food and left, I asked a question.

'Where did you first meet Philip?'

'Philip?' Bob put down his glass. Already he had finished the whisky and moved on to the wine.

'Yes, Philip. Your best man.'

'Oh, Philip!' His voice seemed about to crack. 'Good old Philip.'

I tried again. 'Where did you first meet him?'

'Philip?' His mouth was full. He chewed for a few seconds before taking another swig at the wine. Then he poured out another glass. 'In the war.'

'I know. But did you first see him in Africa, in Italy or where?' I smiled to encourage him.

'Oh no. We met at the barracks. We both joined up on the same day, you see. Wars make strange bedfellows.' Now the voice was low and steady. 'You wouldn't think that Philip and I had a great deal in

83

common. But to be together at that time made us friends.' Then Bob spoke more easily at last. It was a question of comradeship, he said. The war was the first time he and many others (he was sure) had known this. People were killed, of course. This made it worse. Your comrades were killed. But the threat of death ... Perhaps it was partly this that drew them closer – those friends he was speaking of. Some had gone, of course. His brother Charles, for instance. Henry, the one whose parents he (Bob) tried to visit once a year. Henry had been another friend, closer than Philip. Bob looked straight at me. At first, he said, when he had reported to the barracks on that first morning and seen the other recruits he had believed it would be school all over again and he had never enjoyed school, had always felt out of place and longed to be back at Cragham. But of course it was different. The friendships were closer, better, real friendships – and Bob had liked this even though the worst that could happen to you was that much worse, for you knew you could be killed (he had always believed he would not survive the war). Philip had been the joker, the light relief, the comedian who'd kept them all laughing, especially during the weeks of training. They had been a bit cruel to him at times, teasing him, laughing at his first attempts at drill. The trouble he'd had holding his rifle! Good old Philip.

As Bob talked, he drank but ate little, leaving most of the food on his plate. The waiters returned to clear away. Then he stood and looked at his watch. 'Ten o'clock,' he said. 'Do you want to turn in? Look, why don't I go downstairs to the bar and have a nightcap while you get ready for bed?'

He left the room so quickly that he cannot have heard my answer – and I knew now that the moment had come. 'I'm sure Bob will be careful.' My mother's words came back to me and I thought – well, it will be bad – and I remembered from some book or perhaps some story at school that there was supposed to be pain at the start, only a moment of pain, of course. But in the hotel that evening there was no escape from this duty, so in the bathroom I stood in front of the mirrors before putting on the new nightdress. I had hung up the blue suit, folded the blouse and put my shoes neatly together in the tall brown cupboard. I saw myself naked, not so thin (I knew) as I had been a year ago but I hoped interesting to a man – the breasts neatly curved, the rather wide shoulders, a flat stomach, the dark patch between my thighs, the thighs which were perhaps too large above the slim calves and ankles my mother had once said must be the envy of other girls. I knew I did not have much time so I washed, did my teeth, walked out of the bathroom (now wearing a thin pink silk dressing-gown my mother and I had bought at the same shop as the nightdress), took off the dressing-gown and put on the nightdress. Then I did not know what to do. I felt panic. He would be back soon. A drink at the bar. One drink. Most probably a glass of brandy or whisky – something to be gulped down in a minute or two. Then he would come up in the lift, impatiently watching the lower floors pass, anxious to claim those rights which the afternoon's ceremony had given him at last. I was his – this, I saw suddenly, had been the message behind my mother's advice and the way things had been and would be for ever and ever.

In the bedroom I picked up my hairbrush from the small dressing table and began to pull it slowly through my hair, gradually increasing the strength and speed. At first I had to pull hard, then the movement became easier and much quicker, yet even when my hair was obviously free of all possible tangles I still went on, sitting in front of the dressing-table mirror, brushing away. I thought this would be a good position for Bob to find me in when he came back. I would turn round as I heard the door open, arrange my face into a smile of welcome, trying (how I hoped I could do this) not to blush or look frightened. Quickly I put the brush down, reached for the powder puff and had several dabs at my cheeks. No! The clumsily applied powder hung there in spots of absurd whiteness, crumbling a little each time I moved my head. So I rubbed at it, then brushed it off with my handkerchief, leaving what I hoped was a nice pale colouring and was about to pick up by brush again when I thought of a better idea – to lie in bed reading my book, apparently not worried or impatient, although he seemed to have been gone a long time.

Because now I wanted to meet whatever was coming and felt ready for duty or pain or whatever Bob wanted. I was still nervous, yet my mind told me there was no point and this seemed to drive the worst of the nerves away. The sheets of the large double bed were cold. From the table on my side (the left) I picked up my book – a novel by Elizabeth Bowen I had bought three days ago for this week. I read the flyleaf. I liked the romantic title and looked at the name of the person to whom it was dedicated. On the first page, I tried to concentrate on each word at a time, reading slowly, and saw it was a conversation between two people about the feelings of a young girl when I heard the door . . .

He came in, a little unsteady.

'Sorry to be so long. I met a Danish chap who asked me what he should see in London . . .' Then he stopped and looked at me. 'You've turned in. I think I'll do the same.' He stretched his arms up towards the ceiling. 'Is the water hot?' I nodded. 'I'll be with you in a minute.' He opened the chest of drawers, took out a pair of pyjamas and almost ran into the bathroom. I tried to return to my book but the words seemed to mean nothing, as if they were just people talking outside what was real or true. Soon I heard the click of the light switches, first in the bathroom then the sitting room, then the bedroom – and I looked up to see Bob standing by his side of the bed in a thin green dressing-gown and pale yellow pyjamas. I thought I should speak, for I had said nothing since his return from downstairs and I tried a word, not from the book I was reading but one that came from another world.

'Darling . . .'

I stopped. Bob was looking at me. All the tension I had sensed within him entered his face and eyes in a mask of terror – only for a moment though because it went when he spoke, to be replaced by a calmer seriousness. He seemed not to have heard the word and I thought I might have made a terrible mistake in using it. No, what he said was, 'You must be exhausted.' Then he quickly took off his dressing-gown, climbed into bed, turned out his bedside light, lay down with his back to my face and said something I could not hear.

I put down my book. 'Bob . . .' I began, and he turned over towards me, his eyes meeting mine, again desperate, although he was trying to smile, trying (presumably) to make me feel happy. Was this why he put a hand briefly on my shoulder?

'Time for bed,' he said. 'Later . . .'

I moved towards him to hold his hand but again, after a quick turn, the back faced me. There seemed to be no choice. I put down my book, turned out my light and lay beside Bob's silent shape in the dark, with only the sound of regular quiet breathing to tell me that he was alive. Surely he could not have fallen asleep already! I thought of the day, of the crowds, of the dress, of the best man's generous speech, of my father in the car on the way to the church and waiting to take me up to the altar and Bob. Yes, that had been the moment when I had felt that everyone there seemed to want this to happen, that I must be carried forward by this idea which was so strong and true, so inevitable, that it made Bob and I seem suddenly the least of people. No, not that – because they were all watching us, so we were important but as actors playing the parts chosen for us by someone else. Bob was right. Now I did feel tired, so tired that the will to think, even to live, seemed slowly to be pressed out of me. I remember thinking – I must not sleep on my back, I must turn because if I don't I will wake soon and feel uncomfortable and in any case if you sleep on your back you snore (or so I believed) which would disturb Bob on our first night together.

But I was so tired now, suddenly overcome, and the wish to remember left me and I slept that night, forgetting the position in which I lay. Did I dream? Yes, but the dream seemed to meet my memories of the wedding, the reception, the day that we'd just lived through and I could scarcely tell the difference. Had this happened – or was it make-believe? Of course the marriage had taken place – that I knew. But the incidents – each incident that I wanted to remember – ran between the truth and imagined truth as I lay in that bed with only Bob's slow, regular breathing to remind me in the dark of what had really taken place. So I slept, to wake suddenly, aware of a movement. My first instinct was to think that I should be alone and I nearly screamed, only just stopping myself in time, having been fooled by the darkness of the room. And I became conscious of a hand, in that place where I knew it must happen – a hand and a face close to my face and the sound of breathing near to my ear, the breaths coming quickly, with a harsh rasping sound as if they were forced. My mother's words came back to me. 'I'm sure Bob will be careful.'

Then I felt the hand make pain for me, the first pain of our marriage. 'Oh God!' I must have cried out, for Bob said something, a word or two words smothered quickly by the gasps of his breath (he seemed suddenly to find breathing difficult), words that I could not hear. He pulled at my nightdress, I lifted up the lower part of myself to help him, remembering through the pain how I ought to behave and he climbed on to me but not completely into the position I thought he must want, for something happened while my knee was still between his legs and I felt the hardness of his thing against the inside of my thigh (this was my mother's words, the truth Sophie and I had wondered about for years, the romances in books and films – they all meant this). Then it softened and I felt a wetness running down towards my knee as Bob sighed, lay briefly half on top of me, shaking slightly, before rolling off to be at my side.

He said nothing. Within a few minutes I heard the return of the slow breathing which must mean he had gone to sleep, leaving me to lie with what was left, with the mess and a dying sense of shock. I wondered if I should go through to the bathroom and clean myself properly, take off the new nightdress and change into one of the old ones I had brought with me as well. Surely this must be wrong, to leave the marriage bed so soon, and I waited and waited (I think I did cry, but not much) until I saw light through the crack in the curtains. Then, as quietly as I could (hoping his breathing would stay regular) I crept out. And when I came back Bob was still asleep, apparently not knowing I had gone.

'I'm afraid I was a bit tired last night.' This was all he said after we had been called by a maid who told us that breakfast had been put on a small table in the main room of the suite. He put his hand on my shoulder as we lay together, still in bed with the curtains now open to let in the grey morning light, and I smiled, looked into his eyes with what I hoped was love, then thought – perhaps he might have another try. I prayed not. I prayed not so strongly because I feared more pain or disgust and was frightened I might not be able to control myself this time.

'I'm sure Bob will be careful.' I believed he had taken as much care as he could for I was sure he was a kind man, a man who could feel for others. No, it was me or the result of the way I was, my failure as a girl or woman, the fact that I knew or felt nothing. I was worthless to him, I decided, and this was why during breakfast he spoke only of the travel arrangements, of our need to pack quickly and how he should ring the porter as soon as possible in order to be certain of a taxi to take us to King's Cross. We ate fast as he talked, his words (I thought) tactfully hiding his disappointment and regret at having chosen me as a wife. He talked as we packed. At times I thought his voice might be about to falter and I see now that I was hoping for signs of a real Bob – or what I wanted the real Bob to be, a man to whom I could speak about what we had just been through together. A week on the Spey lay ahead – an unknown place, a problem I felt I could never solve. In my mind had been these ideas and hopes, now almost rubbed out by the fear, the mess and the pain. Why couldn't Bob say something about it, then I would speak and surely we could be together at last? So I watched him. I watched him in the taxi when he began to read out the names of some of the shops and the words of the advertisements on the sides of the trams: 'W. G. Elliott: Hosiers' and 'Guinness is good for you'. Perhaps he might try a kiss, perhaps lunge there and then, with a frantic heaving and throwing off of clothes. I had heard that the most extraordinary things were supposed to take place in the back of taxis. Whatever happened I would have to control myself, to surrender . . .

Once on the train, I felt safe. But how long and dark that journey is in my memory, through a grey country without the sun. We read. I went on with Elizabeth Bowen, searching her story of love for some clue as to how I might cope but her characters talk so much and so well and do not have to endure these silences that seemed to surround Bob's words. Bob had the newspapers, some magazines and a book of memories by a retired general under whose command he had been in the war. We ate lunch in the buffet car. At the table, opposite my husband, I tried to be cheerful and spoke of the previous day, of what my father had said to me on the way to the church (something about always being able to depend on him if things went wrong), of Sophie's dress (it had been too tight) and the kindness of the Layburn relations. I laughed and Bob smiled at me. He seemed happy. Perhaps, I thought, he is really in love. Then suddenly, as I was picking up my roll, he reached across and grasped my hand – with the roll still in it – and looked serious and I thought he will say something now, so do not let the roll fall on to the table to distract him for I knew these moments were so precious and could end as quickly as they had begun. 'We were tired last night,' he said. 'Now there will be more time.' He moved his hand down to my wrist and squeezed so hard that I had to clench my teeth not to cry out and could only nod and force a smile as the roll slipped from my fingers.

We went back to our compartment. Soon Bob was asleep, his mouth slightly open, breathing heavily, his face outlined like the head of a statue, not softened in the way that my father's is when he sleeps. The day was still dull when we returned to the buffet for a cup of tea. 'Not at all like summer,' Bob said and then, at the same table we had had at lunch, again opposite each other, I began a speech I had been thinking about during the afternoon while he had been sleeping. It would be marvellous to be so much in the country, I said – first on our honeymoon in Scotland, then at Cragham – because I had grown up in London and had had a city childhood, even the first part in Calcutta when I had been too young to remember – that was when my father was working out there, before he and my mother had decided to come back.

'What did Denis do in India?' Bob asked, using my father's name which rather surprised me, although I cannot think what else he should have called him. He had worked for a trading company, I said, arranging deals, mostly to do with the Far East where he still had some friends, but none of it had ever really amounted to much, so my mother's dream of a place of our own in the country never came true and Sophie and I had had to make do with staying with her relations.

Back in the compartment I hoped he might ask me more, but no, he picked up the general's book and read as the sky darkened further into night. At first I tried to read as well, some more of the novel by Elizabeth Bowen, then thought about sleep when the train began to slow down and I heard a shout of the name of our station. Bob leapt up, to start pulling the cases off the luggage rack and we came to a halt by the lights of the platform. 'I think I can manage,' he said – but a porter came into the compartment to help and Bob gave the name of our hotel, saying they had promised to send a taxi to meet the London train. Outside the air was fresh and as we stood on the platform and the porter walked away from us with the cases on his trolley I took my husband's hand and squeezed it, to get some pressure in return.

I need to remember these details. I want to look through them to see if there was any sign of warning. No, not on the drive from the station when Bob talked to the taximan about the prospects for the fishing and what he could expect from the beat owned by the hotel. Then the arrival at the large Victorian mansion – did this fluster him because he had expected somewhere smaller? But he knew the place already. No, he seemed calm with the proprietor, a small, dark-haired man who took us to our room with large high windows and said he would arrange for sandwiches to be sent up as the restaurant closed at nine o'clock. Would beer be all right? They had a wine list but the head waiter had gone home already and the cellar was locked up for the night. 'Welcome to Scotland,' he said. Bob nodded.

Let me think of the room – high windows, the walls painted cream, dark blue curtains, a tall mahogany cupboard, a chest of drawers, a dressing table with small lamps on it with dim bulbs, a cheap chandelier overhead, a sofa, two armchairs, a low table in front of the sofa, all seemed dim and outside through the window an endless night. The small man pulled the blue curtains, then left. The sandwiches came soon and the beer, brought by a shy girl who rushed away from us as quickly as possible and I thought – I want to be her, going back home to her father and mother, to a nice home and a good night's rest. A nice home? How could I have known this? Of course I did not but was using her as an echo of a secret wish.

We sat beside each other on the sofa. This is right, I said to myself, that we should be here on the sofa. First we will eat, then ... Bob fetched me some water from the bathroom when he saw I did not like the beer.

'Will you go out tomorrow?' I said, again covering his hand with my own.

'I don't want to leave you,' he answered, his voice shaking.

'No, don't worry,' I said. 'I can sleep in and walk down to the river later.'

'Yes,' he answered. 'You must do that. Are you tired?' We ate the sandwiches, then Bob rang the bell. The proprietor himself came to take away the plates and glasses. This is the end, I thought – the end of the waiting, as Bob looked at his watch and stood up to say, 'Why don't I take a turn outside while you get ready for bed?'

That evening I was quicker, more sure of what I should do than in the London hotel. When he returned I had unpacked and finished in the bathroom and was lying in the double bed wearing the second of the two white nightdresses.

'It's a beautiful night,' he said. 'Cold but clear.' I put down my book and smiled at him.

'Bob,' I said, just his name. His eyes met mine, then looked at the floor.

'Yes,' he answered. 'I know.' He picked his dressing-gown out of his suitcase and went into the bathroom. Through the closed door I heard the sound of the lavatory flushing, the running water of the basin's taps, then silence before he entered the room again wearing the thin green silk dressing-gown but without pyjamas, this thin legs bare and white as he walked to the door, turned off the main light and then came towards the bed. He looked at me with what seemed to be scorn. Nothing or no one had prepared me for that look. I felt frightened as the other side of the bed dipped under his weight. Then he reached across my body towards the switch of my bedside lamp, making me want suddenly to sink away from him through the floor and into the earth.

We were in darkness. 'Bob,' I whispered and the hand came in the way I had been expecting and thinking about – thoughts I have not written down here because I do not want to recover quite every moment of those days. Yes, this I was prepared for and the sound of the slithering silk as he took off his dressing-gown, the hand leaving me for a moment to pull at the sleeves. 'Bob' – and the sound of his breathing next to my ear as his head touched mine not in a kiss but a quick drawing together as he pulled me roughly to him, climbed on top of me, his limbs covering mine, so that the dim outline I had seen before in darkness covered me, pressing me down so that I raised my hands to push at his shoulders before remembering that I must be quiet and take what I should know was the point of all this. 'Bob.' I waited, then he swore, a word I did not catch – low and furious. I must have been holding his arm for he tore it out of my grasp and let his whole weight fall on to my chest before slapping me hard once, then again, on the side of my face. The shock seemed to freeze me. In spite of the pain, I don't think I even turned away. But his weight meant that I could not move – this and the blow – so I must have seemed like a dead body when finally I felt him come into me and he rolled off in the same way as the night before.

I could not speak – the pain, the shock. Then he said quietly, 'I'm sorry. Don't worry, please ...' before he slept, peaceful after what he had done. At first I still could not move. Is this the way it must always be, I wondered – the pain and the difficulties of last night and tonight? These next days, weeks, months, years would tell me the answer – and I knew I had to go on with the thing, not to run out now, or not without giving him more of a chance because it was my duty and there must be a hope of something else behind the silence, in those glimpses of another Bob I felt I had seen. In any case to leave now would mean going back to my mother and father and admitting that I had not been able to make the marriage work and surely they must blame me for this because I could never hope to tell them the whole truth.

Then I slept at last. When I woke Bob was already up, getting dressed with the curtains still drawn in order not to disturb me – and I heard his voice, completely relaxed, saying, 'What a wonderful day.' At breakfast in the dining room he talked more than usual but without referring to the night before. He seemed worried about my happiness though and said he was thinking what I would want to do up here in the way of walks or perhaps I might prefer just to sit around and rest. He smiled. He was at his most gentle and it was then that I felt for the first time that power he has of pushing me away from something I want to say or do, of putting up a barrier between me and a set of words or plan of action which seems impossible to cross while he is there. At breakfast and afterwards as we walked round the hotel garden in the sunlight with Bob talking about flowers and plants I could never have mentioned our two nights together – the pressure of his kindness at that moment seemed to force the thoughts from my mind, to drive them away and make it seem improper, crude and wrong to say the words to describe them. He spoke of the garden at Cragham.

'I shall need your advice,' he said – to which I replied that I knew nothing. 'No,' he said. 'On what colours to choose. How to lay them out. I've always been bad at that. You will have your border in the way that my mother had before the war. The one by the little gate. But we'll plan it together.' We had reached a wooden seat beside some azaleas. 'Why don't we sit down? Look at the view out to the hills,' he said taking my arm. 'There's a lot to be done in the house at Cragham. I want you to feel that it's yours.'

That morning in the sun we walked and sat and Bob explained why he loved fishing – its solitude, the combination of peace and excitement, the sort of places it took you to and the beauty of those places, not the killing of the fish at all, although of course it was good to land a big one. He pointed out some of the birds and explained how the day looked to him and if there might be a chance of catching something. 'It's too bright now, with this sun,' he said. 'The best time is in the evening. Would you mind if I went out tonight? I don't want you to be lonely' – and I said of course I did not mind and would be happy to read my book at the hotel. At lunch he talked easily. 'Were Sophie and you close?' he asked. 'You're so near in age. I was three years younger than Charles. When you're young, that's a whole generation – in the nursery and at school. Towards the end we were getting to know one another at last. Then he was killed. Will you walk down to meet me tonight on the river bank? It's not far' – so after dinner I went to meet him, walking across a field near the hotel towards the gate that led to a path to the water. It was beautiful – the light leaving the hills, the great shadows they threw out towards the sky, the stillness, the peace – and then I came upon Bob casting out his line. He heard me coming, turned, smiled and started to reel in, then put down his rod to hold up two large fish. 'Look what luck you've brought me!' he called, laughing with pure happiness and I thought – here I am with the man I love who seems pleased at last.

That night we slept. At first I lay awake, waiting for something but trying to be still in the hope that he might think I was asleep and it would not be fair to disturb me again. Nothing happened. In the morning I woke again to the sound of him from the bathroom. 'It's not such a nice day,' he called out and I could hear the rain.

At breakfast the proprietor came up. 'I hear you were lucky last night,' he said and Bob must have misunderstood him at first because he looked angry, his eyes sharp in that way I know well, before the man began to congratulate him on the two fish.

'Mr Brodie has been running this place for years,' Bob said to me. 'He must know every inch of the river.'

'Aye,' the little man said, 'but to know in your head is not enough. It's a question of using the knowledge in the right way and that's why men like your husband catch the fish. What are you going to do today, Mrs Layburn?' I did not answer.

'What do you suggest?' Bob asked. The proprietor laughed.

'There's a good tweed mill in Aberlour – one of the few places left where you can get most of the old patterns. What do you say, Major? I can arrange for Bill MacKenzie's taxi to take you there.' He winked at Bob. 'Or perhaps the Major wants to take you down to the river to give you a few lessons in casting. But it's hardly the weather for that. Why not take the day off? Give the lady lunch in Aberlour, visit the tweed mill and then get back to the river in time for the evening rise.'

We were driven through the rain by the taximan who dropped us off in the centre of the small town, at another hotel. The small dining room seemed to be full of people but a waiter found us a table for two in one corner, set apart from the noise. I thought – another lunch, another meal, will he say something? Then, after the wine had been opened, while I was talking about

Sophie and her young man in the Civil Service, Bob suddenly broke into my sentence. 'The night before last ...' He reached over with his right hand to hold my wrist, this time in a loose way. I looked at him and shook my head but before I could speak he went on in that deep, soothing voice.

'It must have been the excitement. I don't just mean in the obvious sense. Of course you're very beautiful. But it's more than that. You see, I have this strange feeling. I often wonder if I should have survived the war, if it might have been better for me to have been killed, like some of the friends Philip and I had. Old Philip. But for the war we would never have met. And Henry, the one who was killed.' He looked away from me. 'The first time was bad enough but then to treat you like that up here ...'

He wanted an answer. 'You must talk to me,' I said. 'Please don't worry. I wasn't hurt. You didn't mean it.' He smiled, withdrew his hand and brushed it across his forehead. 'There's so much to look forward to,' I went on. 'Up here and when we get back to Cragham. Don't worry.' And Bob seemed to come out of himself at last and I thought as I listened to him – this must be the real beginning of our marriage. We must stay together, he said. How dreadful it must have been for me over these last two days – the shock and the strain. He would have tried to speak earlier about the way he seemed sometimes either to lose control – like the time he had hit me – or to find himself overwhelmed by other thoughts or a shyness that seemed to turn his feelings to ice. A cold wind blowing across him – this is how it was. He did not like to talk too much about it. Displays of emotion always bothered him in men because such moments seemed to lower the person somehow, to make them seem weak, stripped in some way of their manliness. It was all right for women to talk about these things. Perhaps they were to be envied because of this. He did not know.

At the end of lunch, Bob took my arm as we left the hotel. 'We must go to the tweed place,' he said. 'I want to buy you a present.' The sun had come out and we walked to the shop and chose three different lengths of material and I almost said to the old woman who served us – look at me with my husband. That evening he fished and later I went out on that wonderful walk to the river bank and again he saw me coming from a distance, reeled in his line, put down the rod and held up two salmon. 'Look at the luck you've brought me!' he shouted and I ran towards him and we kissed and I thought I felt a softness or tenderness in the way he held me. Yes, surely this was a new beginning – then, afterwards, in the bed I reached out this time and he did respond quicker than I had expected but he was more gentle, although again it was all over before I had had time to wonder if I should feel some sort of excitement.

This did not matter or did not seem to matter that night. As Bob had said, there was so much to look forward to – a new home, a new friendship, a new life. The next day must be the real start of all this – and when I woke in the morning I still felt the anticipation of the evening before. Once again Bob was in the bathroom – most probably it was this noise that had woken me. When he came out I smiled a him from the bed.

'It's a better day,' he said, 'good for an early start,' and he turned towards his clothes which were on a chair near the window. Now he spoke differently, not at all like the day before, the voice sharp and hard, as if giving orders. At breakfast he avoided my eyes.

'Bob, I am looking forward to going home ...' I began and his stare stopped me.

'Why?' he asked. 'Aren't you happy here?'

I began to say — 'Yes, of course, but as we said there is so much to get on with at Cragham.'

'It must be very boring for you,' he said. 'I see that now.' No, no. I again protested, this place is lovely … 'But that's not enough,' he said. 'I'm sorry. You should have told me before. Of course, we must see that you're properly amused. I'll get Brodie to order the taxi and we'll go for a drive. Is that what you'd like?'

'No, no,' I said — 'please, I love the peace and the walk in the evening to meet you on the river bank. I'd like to get on with my book and sit in the garden. Please, don't feel I want anything else.'

It was too late. He was out of his chair and walking quickly towards the proprietor who was talking to one of the other guests at the door. Mr Brodie ordered the taxi. We went on two drives, one in the morning, the other in the afternoon — each through wonderful countryside but as the rain began almost as soon as we turned out of the gate and lasted for most of the rest of the day it was impossible to see. But I did not mind this — in fact I could have put up with anything if my dreams of the night before had come true, if this had been the true start of our marriage — which it was, although not at all in the way I had hoped, for I see now that the pattern was fixed on that day with the silence.

'How's this?' he said as we drove across a bridge. I answered that it was fine.

At lunch I thought I must say — what about yesterday when you seemed to want to share the truth, isn't that what you want now? Can one day make so much difference to the way you think or did I do something to change your mind? Please tell me and I'll try to put it right, to make it possible for you to go back to the way you once were. But I could not because of his extraordinary, silent pressure and the words he used to draw me away from these thoughts towards matters of far less importance, like the way the food on trains seemed to have deteriorated since the war. Once I began, 'Bob, please ...' His eyes seemed to penetrate the centre of my brain, scattering my words.

'Yes?' he answered.

'Please,' I went on, preparing to change course. 'Please do fish, if you'd like. You really don't have to worry about me. I'll be quite happy ...' He smiled grimly and looked towards the window and the rain.

'You want to turn me out in this, do you?' he said. 'I didn't know my company bored you quite so much.' I shook my head and did not reply and that afternoon he read downstairs while I lay on the bed wondering what to do next.

At dinner Bob talked about the history of his family, the generals, the Viceroy and his grandfather's extravagance. 'My father pulled the place round again,' he said. 'He had to cut right back. It's still difficult. The days of that kind of life are numbered. I give us three years at the most before we have to go.' I forced myself to speak.

'But you did say we might do something to the house – together, and make it our own home, as we want it to be.' He glared at me, those sharp eyes once again reaching into my head.

'What do you mean?' he asked.

'We talked about it,' I began, 'and you said ...' – but I was silenced by a quick shake of the head.

'Perhaps our bedroom can be painted,' he said and looked quite friendly for a moment and I thought – this might be my chance.

'But we must do it together,' I insisted. 'We must choose the colours and the patterns. The way you said we could work on the garden,' and if I was speaking now I would add what I have learned to be true – otherwise what is there for me in the place, that cold dead place, except arranging things around you, protecting you from the world, even worrying about the noise that your own child makes in case you get annoyed and say to me again, 'Give the boy to Beryl. She seems to be the only one who can keep him quiet.'

'The garden?' His eyes were so sharp. 'You will have your border, by the gate. Is that what you mean?' I nodded, feeling I could not go on, that this was not the moment and Bob went back to describing what his father and mother had done to save money. He spoke slowly, so that each word seemed to fit exactly the person, thing or thought it was meant to describe – and I felt the coldness in his voice and the strength that was pressing me down. That night in bed, he turned out his light soon, to turn away from me and sleep. I read some more of Elizabeth Bowen, then slept as well, to be woken by his hand in the early hours of the morning, like on that first night in the London hotel. This time too I jumped with fear, then controlled myself and lay still before I felt his weight on top of me and the wetness running down my thigh, then the relief as he rolled off and lay breathing heavily at my side. I thought – at least it is all over – and I remembered the blows to my head and believed each time I should think myself lucky to have escaped these, if he does not hit me again. The next morning he began what is now a regular feature of our life together – his reading aloud from the newspapers at certain times of the day.

Often I think he chooses them for their nastiness – the story about the Huddersfield murder, for instance, or details of some horrible attack on someone. This is the way he is – and I have to submit, for there is nowhere to run to, certainly not back to my parents in Primrose Hill who are so pleased with a son-in-law like

Bob. The first night at Cragham I thought he was going to hit me. Then we seemed to be able to make love quickly but peacefully, not often but from time to time. Once I had to explain to him about my period. He looked shocked – and soon I missed one, then two, and the doctor said I was going to have a child.

CHAPTER NINE

GEORGE LOFTUS STANDS BY THE WINDOW OF THE OLD library, holding the exercise book. He does not turn the page to go on with the story but looks out at the darkening sky.

'Of course you're very beautiful.'

He thinks of Layburn's words to his young wife and seems to sense the unhappiness, also to feel a great welling up of hopeless desire brought on by these scenes of more than thirty years ago. This should have been their time of discovery, like those weeks in his own life at the university – before the Institute, before he had left home, before Pat. Then a girl called Rose had come into his world and he too had had the time and the circumstances needed for romance.

He looks back and is not surprised to find his desire beginning to die. For Rose had had an extraordinary interest in health foods and diet; she had also a habit of gazing intently into his face as if she wished to get to know every corner and line, every possible expression. Rose! She had said that she loved him. Like Catherine, she had been very beautiful, or striking: yes, striking from a distance with her pale face, brown hair (lighter than Catherine's but darker than Pat's) and tall, thin figure, much taller of course than he was. Then the time should have been right: a student romance one summer in the university and its cathedral city – yet only for a week had he contrived to believe this before he realised that she had chosen him at a party not for his attractions but more as a possible convert to her ideas about the link between diet and astrology or roughage and the stars. Girls like Rose do not exist now, he thinks, with their hazy ideals and complete lack of sexual morality: no, that combination of intense seriousness and personal chaos belongs to the past.

This chaos would have destroyed him. The first night in her lodgings, after a supper of lentils and dried apricots, the plotting of his personal astrological chart and a long session in her bed, he had wondered if he might be on the verge not only of a conversion to her ideas about his destiny but a glorious adventure as well. Then over the next seven days the vision had slipped away. The diet he could take – the muesli, the bran, the nuts, the botched attempts at home baking – and in her passion for the stars he was prepared to see a wish to find some lost mystical enchantment behind the brutality of the present age. What he could not hide from himself was the casual way in which she approached their intimacy, the feeling when he held her in his arms of contact with someone much older, harder and more warped, like a thin, tired woman made up like a girl. He found out too that when he spoke of their friendship people referred laughingly to the effect her high-fibre cooking had had on the bowel movements of numerous others who had passed through her hands.

'And such marigolds.' When he stopped seeing Rose after these seven days of diminishing wonder, term ended and he came home to his parents, back to the simplicity of his mother's love. It seemed impossible to find a version of this which was both romantic and physical, where purity and longing found a balance, where he could see clear beauty. He looks at the portrait of Catherine Layburn, then again at the words in the exercise book. 'I was going to have a child' – and feels a stirring of passionate interest. He smiles. A week in a fishing hotel in Scotland; at first this may not seem full of erotic possibility. But a week alone with a young girl who had goodness and heart and wished to give herself to you in the simple way of an innocent bride – ah, that was a real start to a new world where the dreams of Pat and those artistic geniuses who soared far above Friedrich's theories of iconology and structure became fused into the brilliant sharpness of life itself: then to read of the suffering and to imagine his possible part in her salvation.

There is a knock at the door. Quickly he goes back to the easel and puts the exercise book under a piece of cloth that he has brought with his equipment.

'Come in!'

It is Philip Bligh.

'I'm sorry to interrupt. I couldn't resist coming up to see how you are getting on.'

George Loftus speaks slowly in order to hide any signs of guilt or confusion. 'I think I'll have to take some of the pictures back to London with me. I'd like to take photographs and do some research. I want to ask the advice of my colleagues.'

'I'm sure Bob won't mind.' Bligh walks towards the window. Now he is dressed in a grey tweed suit, a thick, pale blue shirt, a tie of dark blue knitted silk and a pair of expensive lace-up shoes on his small feet. His hand shakes slightly as he points towards the sky. 'How can you work in such bad light?'

George sees that away from the window the room is dark, so dark that he cannot make out the details of his visitor's round, pinkish face and neatly combed strands of thin grey hair until Bligh comes closer to him and they are together beside the easel.

'I've got this.' He points to the portable light he has set up, turns on the switch and immediately the Dutch landscape on the easel is bright in the sudden glare.

'Ah, yes.' Bligh leans forward and peers at the canvas, his eyes narrowing. Then he reaches into the breast pocket of his jacket, gets out his spectacles, puts them on and looks again, this time bringing his head so close that the rim of the glasses almost touches the surface of the landscape. 'To whom will you show them?'

'John Dart, the head of the conservation department. Possibly Dr Friedrich.'

Bligh steps back and turns his head towards George Loftus. They are nearly the same height, the older man only slightly taller, perhaps because he stands so straight in spite of his years. 'Is Edith Parr still there, in the library?'

'Yes.'

'I should ask her to look at this. She has an extraordinary memory.' Bligh shakes his head. 'I'm sure I've seen that landscape in another picture, either in a Dutch gallery or a private collection, by Jan Both or Pynaker or one of those people. Edith might know.'

'I was going to leave that one. I've finished work on it.'

'Have you?' Bligh peers again, then points to a patch of discoloration in the sky. 'What about here?'

He blushes. 'It's not a serious flaw, surely.'

'I should take it if I were you, particularly if you're taking the others. Ask Edith. I will be interested to hear what she says. Now what else has Bob given you?' They walk over to the sofa where the other pictures are propped up with their backs to the room. Bligh lifts the Italian canvas and turns it round, puts it against the sofa again and stands back. 'Ah, I've often wondered about him. Obviously it's John the Baptist – in the style of Correggio. Wouldn't you agree? But that's as far as you or I or anyone else can go. We know there's one like it in Dresden, described as being of the Italian School.' Bligh points at the picture, his outstretched finger quivering in the air. 'I think they're both good copies – the Dresden one slightly better than this – of a lost original. Show this to Edith as well, for old times' sake. She and I spoke of it. I even brought her some photographs which she may still have.' He smiles slyly. 'I wonder what Herbert Friedrich will say. Will you tell me? What does Herbert feel about works of art, do you think? Does he agree with Goethe that they should be life-enhancing? How does he find the notion of ideated sensations or tactile values? Most probably rather out of date. I should imagine him to be more a disciple of Warburg or even Strzygowski.'

'Edith Parr told me that you once worked with Berenson.'

'Edith? So she has discussed me with you, has she?' Bligh lifts his head, turning the previous roundness of his face into a soft oval. 'Yes, Jack Ashton sent me to I Tatti after the war. People are often hard on Mr Berenson now, you know, but he taught me more than I can say. He liked to be compared to Winckelmann – and you may laugh at his vanity. To me, however, the comparison has some value. One had to catch him off stage, so to speak, alone in the garden of the villa or on one of his walks in the hills. Then that extraordinary memory and intelligence seemed to free themselves and he spoke without the suspicion or rancour that were so often there before a larger audience. He was a scholar in the full sense of the word, whatever they may say. Damn Friedrich!' Bligh suddenly raises his voice almost to a shout, then is quiet again, the scarlet in his cheeks turning slowly to a less livid shade. 'Has he never read *The Drawings of Florentine Painters*? Have you?' Bligh does not give George time to answer. 'Think of those long winter days in the Gabinetto di Disegni of the Uffizi, where no truly systematic work had ever been done before. And Friedrich has the nerve to call himself a 'pioneer' because of that tawdry little show of bits of twisted metal and lumps of concrete!'

'The modern sculpture attracted large crowds,' George says.

'Crowds!' Bligh raises his voice again. 'Oh yes, I'm sure it did. Any fool can attract a crowd, if he puts his mind to it. No doubt an exhibition of human anatomy with the entire staff of the Institute standing together naked in the hall would prove an equal success. Why don't you suggest that to him?' George smiles politely and has a pang of lust at the thought of Pat's part in such a display. 'But no matter,' Bligh says. 'What about the rest? There aren't many decent pictures left now, after Bob's father's disastrous sale before the war. Did he tell you about that?'

'No.'

Bligh turns the other two pictures round and looks first at the foxhounds. 'Probably a study for the hunt, I should think, wouldn't you? Very like Wootton, yet another reason for thinking that he must have been the artist. Only lack of documentary evidence prevents one from being sure.' He laughs. 'Bob doesn't care one way or the other, of course. I tried to get Geoffrey Kirk up here to have a look, to see what he thought. He was quite interested in sporting pictures, you know. But there was never time when he was director and then he became ill. Ah, now what about this?' He stares at the portrait of Catherine Layburn. 'Burton at his most romantic.' Bligh takes off his spectacles, puts them back into his pocket and touches the frame gently with one hand.

'Is it a good likeness?'

'Not bad. She had a touch of melancholy.'

'Was she beautiful?'

'Yes.' Bligh seems to have a slight constriction in his throat, for his voice breaks on the word. He turns away, then looks once more at George Loftus. 'Will you forgive me? I have interrupted you – and you want to work. May I propose a walk in an hour or so, at the end of the day? It might clear the head.' And he smiles before leaving the room, his short steps hurried and brisk.

He must go back to his room, just for a short time, to recover from this curious emotion: a feeling of sorrow, yes, but also the sense of a great dark void, an apparent infinity of hopelessness. In the passage he steps to one side to avoid Beryl who is scurrying towards the stairs. She smiles shyly, thanks him and he nods, forcing a word or two out in answer.

It was Beryl who had telephoned him in the last week of Catherine's life, when he had given up hope of seeing her again. 'Can I speak to Mr Bligh, please?' He remembers her words and how her confidence had surprised him. 'This is Beryl here, Beryl from Cragham. Mrs Layburn has asked me to say that she hopes you will be able to come up here to see her soon. She's sorry she hasn't answered your letters but the doctor has told her not to tire herself by trying to do too much. If you can let us know the time of the train, the Major will arrange for you to be met at the station.' Bligh had asked how Catherine was. 'She's not well, sir. You will come, won't you? I hope you don't mind me saying this but I think it might make a difference. She hasn't got much longer now. The Major knows that she's asked me to telephone your London house.'

He enters his bedroom and sits down on the chair beside a small desk that has been put at the end of the bed. The Major knows. They have never spoken seriously about Catherine, not even after the funeral when Bligh had stayed the night at Cragham with Bob, Catherine's widowed mother and the two boys. Then he had expected one of those strange moments of clipped eloquence when suddenly his old friend could summon up powers of reason and feeling in a few short sentences, each word so exquisitely pointed and judged. Instead the talk had been of the mourners who had come up from the South for the day: the Layburn cousins, Catherine's sister Sophie and her husband who worked in the Home Office, various relations whom they had not seen for some time. Catherine's mother went to bed early – she suffered from heart trouble and had to take care – leaving Bob and Bligh downstairs on either side of a dying fire.

That night Bob had appeared different: his dark looks etched thin and sharp against the air, robbed of the more comfortable elegance Bligh had linked to Reynolds or Sargent, now not so English in his grief but more in the melancholy tradition of the great Spanish masters. Bligh had watched him put another log on the fire, then asked how Catherine's mother had taken her daughter's death. 'With great courage,' Bob had replied. 'But she hasn't been well herself for the last year or two.' Then a pause. 'They were different, Catherine and her mother. Catherine could have been happy with very little. Of course she wanted to learn about books and pictures and things like that. But that was all. It may not seem so – but she reached a sort of contentment, as much as most of us are ever likely to find. You knew her well, Philip. Wouldn't you say this was true?' The confidence of this glib misjudgement seemed to leave Bligh with no possible response. Then Bob had stood up to show that it was time for them to go to bed and had appeared to need only the black garb, cloak and sword to have stepped out of a portrait in the Prado.

In the chair beside the desk, Bligh smiles. He is at his old game of tracing likenesses. He thinks yet again of Swann, of how in his first reading of Proust some fifty years ago, at university – before the war, the army, Bob, Juan, Catherine, those other errant boys, before his world formed itself and was still in a mysterious, disjointed state – he had seen himself in the description of Swann's habit of comparing people to the figures or colouring in pictures. Later the coincidence grew in force. Swann, on the outskirts of the circle in the Faubourg St Germain, the habitué of the demi-monde, the artist who had wasted his talent and energy on society. Juan and the boys were Bligh's Odette, these violent and shameful passions the equivalent to the Jewish stigma in Paris at the turn of the century . . .

Bligh draws his chair nearer to the desk. He knows he has been caught between two worlds, that those with whom he has worked – Ashton, many of the people at the Institute, even his old friend Geoffrey Kirk – have laughed at the life that Melissa and others of her kind have given him, the dinner parties, evenings at the theatre and weekends in the country, even his time with the Layburns, although he had tried to tell Geoffrey that they and Cragham were different: more honest, simple, true to themselves, without affectation. Geoffrey hinted often that this took up too much time; why, for example, had Bligh published no more than a few articles when he should have written at least one big book? The irony is, of course, that in Melissa's drawing room, even with Catherine and Bob, he was regarded with awe for his presumed scholarship and this had led them to draw back from a complete friendship: this and their understanding of his dark intimacies where he tried to reach Juan and others but generally met only with maddening desire, obsession, the threat of blackmail and violence, shame, filth, scarcely ever more than a glimpse of release or love.

Bligh takes a pen and his spectacle case from his pocket, puts on the spectacles and reaches across the small desk for a sheet of writing paper. He writes a list of names; opposite each he will put an artist. How often has he played this? It has been his equivalent of games of patience, the crossword puzzles, chess problems or similar solitary amusements. Quickly he joins Bob with Reynolds or Sargent as he has done many times in the past, the cool elegance of Captain Robert Orme's portrait in the National Gallery, then on occasions the fastidious boredom, the hauteur of vanity and decadence, the sated sensuality of Sargent's Edwardian aristocrats. Now all thoughts of grave Spaniards have been replaced by examples much nearer home. Juan, who lives on in his memory, although they have not seen each other for years (the last Bligh heard was that the youth had married an American girl in California), he pairs off with one of Caravaggio's laughing shepherd boys who have that touch of mischief which borders occasionally on spite or evil.

The next name is that of Loftus, the picture cleaner whom Bligh suspects is a disciple of Herbert Friedrich, a man he has always disliked. George Loftus: the small intruder with whom Bob seems to wish to replace Bligh as the unofficial adviser on the Cragham collection – or perhaps to use as a way of causing a little discomfort, even pain. Bligh taps the paper with his pen. Loftus is so insignificant, without any apparent outstanding feature other than his lack of height, the face like a million others, neither handsome nor ugly but from the vast middle area of humanity where one person standing in a bus queue or on the Underground is only different to the other because of his or her size or age. Then he has an idea: surely the boy belongs in a crowd, so Bligh writes down Frith or Maclise, seeing George Loftus as one of the mass of racegoers on Derby Day or a sailor at Trafalgar on the occasion of Nelson's death.

He allows the dead to participate in this game as well. Now he has reached Catherine, always a difficult person to pair off because she does not seem to belong to the past, or not to the grand past of the great portrait painters; her beauty is too comfortable, too sympathetic, without any of the remoteness or self-regard of posed studies. Bligh finds himself thinking yet again of the pre-war Bohemian world of Augustus John and the cult of the natural and the free. Of course, this had been as self-conscious as any life it had sought to replace and Catherine would not have been at ease there – but often she had seemed to point a way forward from inhibition and fear, not so much by what she said as through an example of simplicity and the beautiful wish to seek out the truth. Surely there had been freedom on those summer afternoons in the garden here with her children and the warmth of the time she and Bligh had known together, and perhaps the days with that other man.

Bligh thinks of those John drawings of gypsies, the mothers carrying their babies at their hips: the casualness of the scene's beauty. Yet how absurd. Catherine had not been at all Bohemian, not at all easy or adventurous. Bligh leaves the space blank against her name. He thinks he knows the limits of her experience. He remembers how at the funeral he had looked at the mourners to try to fit each one into her life: her mother, Bob, the boys, Beryl, himself, her sister Sophie, her cousins from Gloucestershire, the Layburn relations, the Blagdens, other friends and neighbours. There was only one man missing, the great gap in Bligh's knowledge of her, the person who knew more than anyone else, the reason why he is still not sure if he has understood her at all.

CHAPTER TEN

In the old library, George Loftus has gone back to her journal.

Since the birth of Charles, Bob has not bothered me so much in bed. No, I don't quite mean that – because sometimes up here in the afternoons my thoughts become muddled and I seem to see him differently to the way he really is.

I could see he was pleased about Charles, I suppose at least partly because I had produced an heir to Cragham which must be one of the things he wants. He must be pleased – and he did say so in the hospital at last when one of the nurses congratulated him and asked what the baby was going to be called. Charles. Bob did not even need to think before he said the name that has been in the Layburn family for generations, stretching back through his dead older brother, his grandfather, then the Viceroy and the generals as well.

I am trying to write down now what I have come to know about my husband because it seems a way of getting through these long long afternoons. Apparently I am not one of those women who find it easy to have children and at one moment the doctors were worried although they tried hard not to show it. I have told people this – not exactly in those words but I have said that the doctors have advised me to be careful for the moment and to try to rest for a part of the day and that this is nice because it means I have more time to read and Beryl is so good with the baby that I need not worry at all.

So I have my book. Sometimes I stick photographs into one of the two big leather albums Bob's aunt gave us, photographs of the wedding, then the time in Scotland and those first few months here in which Bob always manages to appear serious but kind with a straight look and a slight softening of the eyes so that he seems to show love for me through the camera. When Philip Bligh came here for the first time after our marriage I showed him some of the snaps and he said, 'Bob looks so happy, so at ease with the world.' He likes to think of the future and the albums on the shelves of the old library alongside those from the Viceroy's time, a record of what life was like here when we were starting out on our years together.

I felt badly about Philip – well, not about him personally but about the way I let myself go with him and talked and talked and talked. Of course, it began in that restaurant after the concert at the Institute when he told me about Juan and he seemed so possessed by the boy that I could not interrupt for I felt the chance to get this off his chest meant so much that to have to stop might have done something terrible to his reason. Later he admitted he had said all this to me partly because we did not know each other at all well and also because I seemed ready to listen without wishing to pry or ask awkward or what he calls 'literal' questions. Didn't he think I might have been shocked, I wondered? Yes, Philip answered – but not until afterwards because the trouble with Juan had been so fresh in his mind that he thought he might have poured it out to the first person he had found himself alone with for more than ten minutes. Then he started to talk about the boy again and his voice took on that strange tone I had noticed before in the restaurant on the day after the concert – as if he had almost forgotten I was there and was speaking to himself, the words at times not very clear as he stumbled for a moment or seemed to find it difficult to breathe.

Poor Philip! I must try to write down some of the details of this second talk. He came to stay at Cragham towards the end of our first winter there when I was having Charles. There was no one else – just Philip, Bob and me – and it wasn't nice enough to spend much time outside, so on the Saturday morning we sat in the drawing room in front of the fire while Bob was busy downstairs in the gun room with his letters and other work he said he had to catch up on. 'Will you excuse me?' he asked Philip in that polite way he has from time to time when he bends slightly towards you (generally Bob is taller than almost everyone else in the room, no matter how many people are there). 'Will you excuse me? Philip, I commit my wife to your care,' and then he bowed and smiled before leaving the room.

At first I wondered if this would work, if Philip and I would be able to talk naturally, for it was the first time we had been alone together since the concert. Since then he had written to me twice, once only a day or two after our talk and the second in answer to my letter in which I had asked him to come up here whenever he wanted. I did not try to tell him any more then, partly because I felt incapable of dealing with the ten or fifteen pages of apology of his first letter. 'How could I have lost control of myself to such an extent?' he wrote – then went on to say he would understand if I never wished to see him again and all he had really wanted to say at the lunch was how good he felt I was for his old friend Bob Layburn, how marvellous it was to see Bob so happy – and then something had happened to loosen his tongue in this terrible way. I was too kind, too sympathetic, too sweet.

That morning in the drawing room it was easier than I had thought. At first we talked about the weather and how sensible it was of Bob to get up to date with his letters and soon Philip started to apologise again, using almost exactly the same words as he had in his letter. Then he went back to the subject of Juan, taking his eyes off me as he spoke of treachery, betrayal and the morals of the gutter. These were some of the words he used, his voice again trembling and I felt it extraordinary that someone could be so completely obsessed with another person, so obsessed that he seemed to hate to be reminded of Juan – as was shown by the way in which his whole face seemed almost to explode when he used the terrible and violent language – yet to want to talk about nothing else. 'But you must see,' Philip said to me 'you must see what I mean.' I wondered – why should I see because I have not known and cannot really imagine what it is to feel like this? I did not want to pry, yet I did wonder then about what had gone on between them, not so much in the way that Philip had adored the boy and the boy had just seen Philip as a useful source of help and money but more about how Philip's love had shown itself and what they had done together.

'You must understand,' Philip said. I said I did, although the thought was going through my head that this was far beyond anything I had known or ever could know and then suddenly I could hold it no longer and I answered, 'Why do you think I should?' Philip stopped at last, perhaps shocked for a moment before he smiled in a gentle way and he does have the gentlest smile of any man I have ever met, even more gentle than my father's when Sophie and I used to find him alone. 'With Bob,' he answered. 'You seem so much in love.' I did not know what to say and luckily he went on. 'I can't forget that time I saw you a few months ago at that dinner party in London. The way you were with each other, those quick, true, beautiful looks across the table in the midst of all that affectation – the empty chatter of a rotten world.' Here again his voice shook for a moment before regaining its balance, although he seemed to have to speak slowly for the next few sentences before the words began to flow again at their usual speed. 'The mess of those people's lives – or what they have allowed their lives to become,' he said and looked straight at me, no longer towards the window. 'The two of you seemed like a fast, strong current running through it all – Bob's courage and strength, your beauty and the news about the child. You must be careful, Catherine. Don't try to do too much over these next few weeks. It would be terrible if there was an accident of some kind. Bob would be devastated.'

Then I gave him a small glimpse of the truth because I could not bear someone to be so out of touch with what was really happening to me – someone I was beginning to look on as a friend in spite of the short time we had known each other. 'He would?' I asked. 'How do you know? Has he told you?' Philip looked surprised and began to say that it was not necessary to be told – surely I could see my husband's happiness, the proud way he looked at me. 'Can you see these things?' I asked. Why, yes, Philip answered and said that he knew Bob well enough to be able to sense his moods and the state of his mind and surely I . . . He was quiet for an instant – then he gave another of those gentle smiles and asked in a voice that was lower than usual. 'Is something wrong between you?'

I feel terrible about how I very nearly gave way at

that point and released it all. But I cannot help thinking of what I might have said — how Bob seems to be someone who is full of self-love, how I felt then and still feel now that in the end he does not care if I live or die as long as he is not put to too much trouble by my death or illness. Perhaps I might have told Philip of that evening when we were in our bedroom or rather I was there lying in bed waiting for Bob while he undressed in the room next door that he uses as a dressing room. Perhaps I should go and surprise him, I thought – and try to say something at last, yes why not and I got out of bed and went to the open door between the two rooms quietly so that he could not hear. There he was holding up a jacket on a hanger, flicking at the shoulders with his other hand to make sure that the dust and the moths had not been able to do any damage. There, lined along the floor of the open cupboard out of which he had taken the jacket, were those two rows of shoes with wooden shoe trees inside them to preserve the shape and the leather, each pair polished a bright brown or black in the way that he liked Beryl to do. Even in the hotel in Scotland on our honeymoon he had been particular about his shoes, leaving them outside the room every evening so that they would be cleaned and ready for him to wear the next day.

Then he turned and saw me. I cannot forget that look, first of anger, then I am sure of hatred just for a split second but long enough for me to see and to start to back away as he came towards me. He dropped the jacket and had his right hand raised in the air and I thought – my God, he is going to hit me and beat me now, much worse than he had ever done before and I am here alone with no one to help and I must run somewhere to another room, another part of the house, lock myself in but he has all the keys in that bowl in the gun room so the only safe place is outside, away from him. Yes, I would run to one of the cottages at the end of the drive, perhaps to Beryl's family, although I knew that they looked upon Bob as someone who can do no wrong, so most probably it would be better to run on and on in my nightdress into the cold night, the stones of the drive cutting into my feet, then the low branches of the trees and the thorns of the bushes bringing me down in the woods so that I could go no further and must wait for the sound of his slow footstep coming after me as he followed my trail.

But Bob did not attack me that night. No, his hand dropped to his side and the violence in his eyes turned to that hard bleak stare. 'What are you doing?' he asked. 'You must go to bed. The doctor has warned you that if you're not careful you will lose the child.' So I went away.

Of course, I did not tell Philip about this but I gave an answer which took him nearer to my real life. 'I must learn how to talk to Bob,' I said. 'Please tell me. How do you think I might get closer to him?' Philip's smile did not change as he asked me what I meant. 'I mean from almost every point of view,' I answered and he looked awkward for a moment. Please say more, I thought. I wished him then to say more and I hoped my wish might reach into his mind.

It must have done because almost immediately he asked a question, still awkward but clear enough for me to understand. 'In Scotland, when you stayed together in that hotel, was it the first time for you both?' Then he reached out his hand quickly as if to reassure me – the chairs were too far apart for our hands to meet unless one of us stood and walked towards the other – and said, 'Please, if this embarrasses you – please don't answer – but sometimes it can help to talk these things over with a friend, someone you can trust. It's the least I can do after troubling you with so many of my own problems.' I said yes it was but that had not mattered – I thought I had to add this because I suddenly felt the shame, something I seem to have with the truth about Bob and me, my strange wish still not to betray him. Why should I spoil Philip's unreal ideas, his belief that his old friend was so happy, so in love and looking forward to being a father, so pleased with me? And I thought Philip knows nothing at all about this man who is supposed to have been close to him since those days in the war. 'I'm sure Bob was careful,' he said. 'Or is that what you mean when you say you cannot get close enough to him?' Then I felt the pressure from Philip, the way he was trying to will me to say more, to take him right into the heart of our marriage, almost into the bed itself – first in London and later in that Scottish hotel.

So I stepped back from giving any more hints or even the smallest detail, yes, I pushed Philip away from our life together and said, no this was not what I had meant at all – and then asked how he thought I might best be of use to Bob in this house, perhaps by taking the trouble to learn about the pictures and the building and the whole history of the place so that all that side of things might become my responsibility from now on and Bob would refer anyone who wanted to know about it to me and I could answer their letters or questions myself. The trouble is, I went on, that I have had no proper education at all, just a few years at a girls' school in London chosen by my mother because she thought it was suitable – so I will have to be taught and I want to learn about other things as well – like books and music and those great gaps in my life, although I do read in rather an unplanned sort of way. Would he teach me, would he be my guide? I could only ask him but of course I did not want to take up too much of his time.

That was how my affair with Philip began. He might laugh to see me describe our friendship in this way but it is how I think of us. Would he help me? 'Yes,' he said, 'of course I will' – and I began to ask about the things in the drawing room and we stood up to look at the pictures together. At first his answers were short, with as few words as he could get away with – or so it seemed to me, and I could feel the pressure still of his unspoken wish to take us both back to the way we had been talking only a few seconds ago. But I pushed against this, trying to coax him away. 'I wish I could come to your lectures at the Institute,' I said and he laughed. We had reached the large picture of the hunt, one of the largest pictures in the house and I asked about this and at last he spoke of the classical landscape and the artist's wish to mark the death of General Layburn, a great national hero, by painting him here in the land of his ancestors with his beloved hounds and a few close friends.

Philip turned to me. I asked if it would be possible to see that stretch of country. 'The view is mostly from the artist's imagination,' he said, 'although he may have taken a few features from a real landscape.' Can we look, I said – perhaps this afternoon in the car? I was sure Bob wouldn't mind, that he would be busy with something at the farm or with some county council work or one of his local causes. We must go on a search, I insisted, and he agreed to come and we laughed together and I felt we had both decided to hatch a secret plot, something that involved only the two of us with the rest of the world left out.

At lunch Philip asked Bob about his morning and was told of the letters which still needed to be dealt with, although he had managed to get through some in spite of the fact that the telephone had rung several times, once a call from the vet to say it was time for the dogs to be looked at again. 'The dogs?' I asked. Then I repeated the word to show that I had been paying attention to what Bob was saying and also had not remembered the strange illness which had attacked the dogs a month or two ago – when they had seemed to be forever scratching themselves and leaving tufts of hair all over the place – that illness Bob had spoken about so often at the time that it should have been engraved on my heart. 'Yes,' Bob said, 'the dogs,' and his words seemed to be forced through a barrier of anger, even of hatred – for I am sure that he must hate me because he never shows me any other feeling, or so it seems at times. 'They nearly died last month. Do you remember?'

Philip tried to help. 'Catherine and I were thinking of going on a drive this afternoon, Bob, to see if we could find some of the features in the landscape of the hunt. Have you any idea where it might be? Why don't you come with us? Leave your desk for an hour or two at least.' Bob smiled, now a perfect example of courtesy. He said how kind it was of Philip to suggest such an expedition, although he doubted if we would find much of significance because the countryside around here had suffered a great many changes since the industrial revolution. Indeed, he feared that the General might be shocked were he to come back and see the result. Then for a moment Bob seemed to become excited. The old way of life might return, he declared, as the factories and collieries closed one by one and then perhaps the view in the picture could begin to emerge out of the newly restored landscape, like a pearl out of a dark sea – and he smiled again at the end.

'Why don't you come with us?' Philip asked once more, but Bob shook his head. No, he answered, he must get on with his work – and as he smiled again I laughed, partly I am sure because I was so pleased to see him calm and easy again – then he turned on me with all the humour out of his eyes to say, 'I see you don't believe me.' Before I could answer, he was talking again to Philip, asking who was to drive the car and if we knew exactly how to get where we wanted to go – and Philip had not noticed my discomfort at all, to judge by the quick way he smiled at Bob in return and said that as it was my car he was sure I should take the wheel.

'Oh, it's Catherine's car, is it?' Bob asked with that laugh that might have implied a tease to Philip but to me meant anger. 'I wonder which she means – the one I bought a year ago or the one I paid for last month. Which of those cars is hers do you think? Perhaps she would like to tell us.' I said that I had been thinking of the small blue car I used for going into the town or whenever I needed to go anywhere and that he had said it was mine (my voice sounded strange, to show I was upset and again I thought – at least Philip will notice). 'I see.' This was his answer with that slight bow of the head. 'You will remember to be careful, won't you?' Then he turned to Philip. 'The doctor has told her to take great care, particularly in these first months. Will you see that she is sensible, if only for her own sake?' He laughed, then left and I was about to say to Philip, 'Do you see now?' but thought Bob might decide to come back to fetch something and would catch us talking about him so instead I said, 'I really don't feel at all ill, just a bit sick in the morning sometimes and rather tired – but life is so quiet up here that there's plenty of time to rest.'

I loved that afternoon. Philip talked most of the time but I must not make it seem as if he gave me a series of long lectures because he talked only in reply to my questions and I said at one moment in the car when we had reached the crossroads where the park wall ends,

'What a wonderful teacher you must be!' We found nothing, or nothing we could definitely point to as part of the landscape of *The Cragham Hunt*. But it was the real start of my affair with Philip. On the way back I said I would never have seen even a quarter of what he had pointed out to me in that picture and how was it possible to reach inside the artist's mind and know what he had meant, to which Philip answered that he was merely interpreting the work in the light of the customs and symbols of the time, not trying to recreate the man's thoughts – to do that it was necessary to be an artist oneself, a creator, and great writers like Dostoevsky, Proust and Thomas Mann had tried to explain the creative mind. He would tell me the names of some of the books to read and this was how we began that scheme which was going to give me the education I had never had – with Philip as my teacher as well as my friend. Not even Bob's grim face in the hall when we returned and his order that I should sit down until dinner to avoid tiredness or strain – not even these could stop my excitement at the thought of these months and years ahead for Philip and me together when I would learn all he could give to me, and I paid no attention but walked straight into the drawing room to have another look at the great picture beside the door.

Then I wished Philip could live with us. That evening as we sat together in the drawing room after Bob had gone back to the gun room and his letters or business I told him this and he laughed and said, 'No, we should not meet too often if we wish to remain friends.' I could not believe this – stay on, I said: if only for two or three days more but Philip answered, 'You forget about my work' – so the next morning I drove him to the station and we both went on to the platform to wait for the London train and just before he got into the carriage we kissed, this time for longer than the short touch on the cheek he had given me when he arrived. Then I went back to my car and drove to the house alone, feeling the child move inside me as if to say that I was fixed to Bob now because of my condition and it was wrong of me to think badly of him for wanting me to take care.

Philip and I went on writing to each other. He suggested books for me to read and said that I must give my honest reaction, not what I thought I should feel – and I did read them, then wrote back. At first I was frightened of making a fool of myself but soon I started to think on my own. These letters became very important to me. Each morning I would come down and go through the post to look for that envelope – and I could expect to see it most days because Philip wrote to me certainly three times a week, often four and sometimes even five or six so that there were periods when we were in touch almost every day. He hardly ever telephoned, I suppose because he was frightened that Bob might answer and he must have known how much Bob hates the telephone and might be angry with us both. In any case, what could Philip say, what excuse could he have for wanting to speak to me?

Often there was a silence in the house during those months of spring and early summer while I was growing larger with Charles. Even at meals Bob sat sometimes with a newspaper or farming magazine in front of him, saying that this was the only time he had to read and in the evenings when you would have thought we might have sat together he usually went to the gun room to answer letters. At this time he was improving the garden – so every weekend he was out there on his own with an axe and a saw, unless the weather was too bad, in which case he would go again to the gun room and his letters and his gardening books which he used to help him draw up great detailed plans of new groups of shrubs and trees. I remember looking out of the window on a warm Saturday in May to see him beside some rhododendrons by the path on the way to the gate, stripped to the waist – standing for a moment to rest, leaning on his axe, his dark hair wilder than usual, and I suddenly thought – how magnificent he looks, yet why is his strength turned on these trees and plants in the fierce, almost crazy way I have seen him attack the rhododendrons which he says he wants to destroy? Remember me, I almost called out from the house as he swung the axe and brought it down on to the tree – remember me, but even if he had heard my voice from that distance it must have been drowned by the noise of the splintering wood.

A silence fell on our life together. After I told Bob I was going to have a child, he drew even further away from me, no longer wanting even to try to make love. At first I found this a relief, especially as I was heavy and sick and tired at times in those early months but then I started to feel the loneliness and the memory of those awful sessions at the start of our marriage was pushed aside by the wish for closeness of almost any kind. Probably he no longer found me desirable in my new state, probably he found my size disgusting and I did not dare approach him on my own because I could not imagine what he might do. He noticed some of the other changes in me, the way that strange books were often by my chair in the drawing room. Several times he picked up one of these and I would ask if he had read it and he would generally say yes but a long time ago and then make it clear that he did not want to talk any further on the subject. I tried to draw him out, once on Turgenev I remember, when Philip had told me about the great Russian writers but then all Bob said was, 'Yes, he is good,' before again making it clear that the subject was closed, leaving me to wonder if my husband might be like those squires of the steppes who had been a law unto themselves, leaving their wives and neighbours to cope with them as best they could, more marvellous probably to read about than to know. By his bedside there were only those books about gardening.

This was why the letters were so important. I tried to use what Philip taught me in all parts of my life. When the house opened to the public in April I asked the guide to tell the visitors about the details of the big picture of the hunt and repeated what Philip had said about the classical landscape and the signs of mourning for the General – but she apparently spoke to Mr Gatehouse, the agent, who spoke to Bob, who told me not to confuse everyone with these theories from books because we must keep things simple for the public and it was better to leave the arrangements for the opening to Mr Gatehouse who had been dealing with these matters for years and knew all the drill, so on the two afternoons a week when the ground floor is open I lie upstairs in my room and hear the public come – not many because Mr Gatehouse says few people take their holidays in this part of the world and of those who do even fewer come out here – and the high voice of the guide not clear enough for me to get the words. I think I could tell them more but I am not allowed to because I am a prisoner in my own home. What would they say if I rushed into the drawing room to shout this and to speak about us, the people who live here – what if I told the truth?

How I longed for Philip to come back. Of course, there were other guests from time to time as there have been since the start of our marriage, although I know Bob would much rather be alone. Once he said when the Blagdens were coming soon after our return from

Scotland, 'I don't know why we need them,' and I had seen this as an attempt to say we would have been much happier just with each other but now I see he was thinking of time lost in the garden and the break in his sacred routine. Yet Bob is always good to the guests. Sometimes when there are people I look down the dining-room table at him and see why I fell in love and remember the dance in Gloucestershire and the evenings in London and his mystery and those dark good looks and his smile which is the way he is with his friends. That first time the Blagdens came after our marriage did encourage me, on the Friday evening when he seemed so kind and Tony Blagden said what Philip had also said, 'Bob looks happier than I have ever seen him before.'

On the Saturday afternoon, while Bob and Tony were out shooting pigeons, Liz Blagden had sat with me in the drawing room. 'Tony was really Charles's friend,' she said, 'Bob's older brother who was killed.' I told her that it had been awful for Bob because they were very close and most probably he would never really get over it and this was how deaths could affect some people for the rest of their lives. 'Has he told you that?' she asked. Liz Blagden smokes – and she watched me as she drew on her cigarette. 'Tony tells me they fought like a couple of tomcats when they were boys – or that's what he remembers. Bob never lets any of us get close, does he? But you seem to have managed it. I hardly knew Charles. But he was different to Bob – more casual, less serious, I suppose. All the girls were in love with him – and with Bob but for different reasons.' She looked hurt for a moment. 'Bob had a good war, didn't he? I like a man with guts. You're lucky, Catherine. Mind you look after him.' Then she repeated that phrase. 'I've never seen him look so happy. Ah, here they come' – and we went through to the kitchen to fetch the tray on which Beryl had laid out the tea.

Philip was the only person who could help me. This was why I longed for the summer and his next visit. I urged him to try to come sooner – even if only for a day and a night – and offered half as a joke to pay the cost of his journey but he wrote back to say there was too much for him to do at the Institute to allow any chance of a break – he had lectures, classes and seminars most days of the week and he was trying to finish an article which had been promised months ago and the publishers were asking yet again about the book on Venetian painting. I envied him this when all I could give in return was my opinion of a book or the story of another visit by the Blagdens or my parents or Sophie and her new husband or a Saturday lunch with Colonel Cochran and his wife Barbara, our neighbours who have the farm on the other side of the hills and I felt I should end each letter – this is all there is to me now, please make allowances for this, if only we could talk there would be much more to say I am sure.

He came in August. By then I had grown much larger with the baby. 'You look wonderful,' were his first words on the station platform, for I had driven to meet the train in spite of the heat of that late summer day – and I had to hold myself back from pouring it all out to him there on the station as we kissed and I felt myself starting to laugh and cry at the same time. In the car it was the same, so much so that I dared not speak and we found ourselves talking about his journey and the discomfort and how the trains seemed to run much more smoothly before the war. I suppose I was looking for too much from the visit and I should have thought about the time that had passed and how his life must have moved on, although mine had remained the same – but Philip's manners are too good for him ever to show this. Towards the end of the first day in the cool of the evening we sat in the garden. Bob had gone to look at one of the ponds in the wood on the edge of the park, striding off in his shirt sleeves with the dogs behind him and Philip had waved goodbye from his seat beside me on the lawn.

I thought then again – how can I start because there is so much to say and yet when the moment comes I reach for the words and know it must all sound so small? So I asked how he was and he said he felt tired. These last months had been particularly hard because Geoffrey Kirk had asked him to take over some of the duties of a colleague who was ill – and Philip did look pale, his skin dead round his face where he had put on weight. 'But that's been my only problem,' he said. 'Just work. At least it takes one's mind off other things' – and I presumed that he meant there were no more difficulties with Juan, that the boy had gone. 'And you?' he asked. 'I love your letters. You will keep writing to me, won't you? How much longer now till the birth? Two months? Three?' I told him that the baby was due in September. 'Please,' I said. 'You must write to me as well.'

Then we spoke about his work and he tried to explain what he had been doing and from there we moved on to some of the books he had told me to read. 'What does Bob say?' Philip asked. 'Does he notice?' – and I said that he had seen the Turgenev. 'He did read, you know,' Philip said. 'I'm sure I remember, in the war . . . How is it now? Would you like to tell me?' I did not understand. 'I mean between the two of you,' Philip said. 'You've hardly mentioned Bob in your letters.' His look was so eager that something about it made me draw away and remember Bob's face at its most gentle and interested when we have guests or when he is talking about some plant in the garden or animal or bird so that I felt I must not betray him now and I answered that everything was fine. We were both looking forward to September and the birth so that I might return to a normal life.

Philip was with us for four days but this was the only time we came near the truth. He pressed me once or twice that August and I did not dare to give even the smallest hint because I thought I might not be able to control myself once we began to talk and I could cry or collapse. The weather changed to rain on the second day – and when he left the sky was dark and I looked back on the walks we had had and the hours in the drawing room and the old library getting on with what Philip called my 'education' or just listening to me talk about my mother and father and my life before I married Bob and then the baby and if I minded if it was a boy or girl – I looked back on this and wondered why he could possibly want to come here again. As we said goodbye, I noticed his kiss was not so warm as on the day he had arrived and he turned quickly to get into the carriage with his bag.

Philip has not been back since then. We still write and I told him all about Charles's birth in September and he sent flowers to the hospital and some more for me when I came home with the baby. Now it is March and I sit writing this in my room and life is the same and Bob tells me that Colonel Cochran and his wife Barbara and their daughter Rachel and her husband are coming to lunch tomorrow. I hear the baby crying upstairs. What can Beryl be doing to him?

George Loftus looks at the portrait. He thinks: yes, I would have her here amongst these books and the reminders of this house's past, slowly and gently — for this is surely what she needs and her beauty would seem wonderful and glorious in the beauty of the place and together we could forget our own troubles and the heartbreaks of the world.

CHAPTER ELEVEN

THERE IS A GAP IN THE EXERCISE BOOK, THEN THE writing begins again and he goes back to her life.

My father is ill. I heard this morning when my mother rang from London. She would not talk much, saying she was sure it was nothing to worry about. He had a turn in the night and felt strange, so she called the doctor who told him to stay in bed for several days. It means they will not be able to come here which is rather a relief, although I know they want to see Charles again and it seems unkind of me to be pleased that they will now probably not come until the summer. But this place has such an odd effect on my mother. She seems to pose in the drawing room, throwing her head back in a way that she feels is right. She asks after 'the staff' – as she calls them – and talks loudly about her unmarried days when she went to grand parties and stayed in big houses before the war.

This is not the first of these turns, although she does not like to admit it – and each time he goes to bed for a few days, then gets up to go out somewhere, partly I think to get away from her for a short time. This is all he can hope for now. When he comes here he seems shy and lets her talk and tell us what they have done or seen together, also what he thinks, and I wonder if he has not really died years ago and these illnesses are only the outward signs of a body that lives around a dead spirit. When they see Charles they are sweet to him. At last my mother is natural and stops talking to Bob about his ancestors or the Viceroy or how she once met Lord and Lady Willingdon in Calcutta before the war when my father worked there which was fascinating, although they had decided to come home because it would be better for the girls to grow up in this country.

The baby seems to please us all. In the hospital, with the troubles after the birth, the feeling that he was there brought me through all the pain and sadness and I wanted to get him home, away from everyone else. How cold the house was when we returned. Bob drove us back from the hospital and helped me upstairs, then stayed to see I was comfortable in bed before he left to go to the gun room. At first I hoped he might move out of the bed to his dressing room next door, then I felt ashamed of myself for thinking this – because Charles is just as much his son as mine and why should he not sleep where he wants?

It was mostly the cold that got me down, I am sure – the cold of the house and that room. Although Bob put an electric heater in there it seemed to make hardly any impression on the damp cold air and every night there was a frost which brought the temperature down even further. At first the baby slept in the room with us and I woke in the night to feed him and I knew Bob didn't like this, even though he made a show of not minding the first two or three times – but he never suggested another way of arranging things, just moving away from me when I turned on the light and hardly looking at the little boy as I put him to my breast. Charles often would not go to sleep after I had fed him but cried and I had to try to quieten him down by walking around the room in the terrible cold, wearing

my dressing-gown, hearing Bob's breathing and thinking – surely he can't be sleeping through the noise yet
even when Charles woke at other times in the night
Bob would just turn his back on me and seem to go
back to sleep straight away. I was so tired during those
first days I could hardly think.

Beryl saved me, I suppose. It was the doctor who
spoke to Bob about my condition becoming worse and
said I must have more rest or I might break down. I
was sitting up in bed at the time and we were all
together in the bedroom – Dr Maltby, Bob, the baby
and me. 'There must be one warm room in the house,'
Dr Maltby said and then Bob suggested that Beryl
should come and live in and the old nursery should be
opened up and heaters put in it because it faced south,
so did not get quite so cold. She had been a nanny with
some other people for a short time before coming to
work for us in the kitchen. The child cried with me,
Beryl said, because he was not getting enough milk and
we must take him off the breast as soon as possible, so
she mixed up the bottle and took him upstairs to sleep
with her at night. At first I wanted to be there for the
night-time feeds – so I set my alarm clock only to find
that Beryl had already fed him or I could not make
him take the milk either from me or the bottle, so I
had to hand him over to her because she seemed to be
the only one who could calm him down. So my breasts
started to go dry and Charles will never be with me in
that way again.

I had to fight for my child. Bob and Beryl and the
doctor seemed to be plotting against me, using the
excuse of my health to take Charles away. When he
was with me and seemed at all upset in the way I know
babies often are Bob would hear the crying and come
through to say I must call for Beryl – either this or he
went upstairs himself and sent her down and she would

come into the room looking so meek and polite but determined to do her duty to the Major, as she called Bob, and make sure that his son was properly looked after. Sometimes I thought then I would refuse to give the child up to her, even in front of Bob. I would make a scene, I thought, and lie down on the floor holding on to Charles and they would have to force him out of my hands – but I knew I could not stand the noise and the struggle and the pain as the crying turned to screams and they both went ahead, doing their best to obey the doctor's orders. 'You're lucky enough to have someone to help you, Mrs Layburn,' Dr Maltby had said. 'You've had a difficult time. Now you must rest to regain your health and then you will be able to enjoy your baby.'

I must do what he says. I know they are thinking of me and trying to help. They watch me all the time now – this morning for instance when Beryl and I bathed the baby together and I held him in the basin she was ready with her hands, waiting for me to let him slip or fall into the water so that she could seize Charles from me and know he was safe again for Bob. I thought then as I looked at her – I have so little I can call my own, now they are taking my child and my father is going to die but it is best for me, as the doctor says, and I gave the baby to Beryl after the bath and went to the kitchen to get things ready for these people who were coming to lunch.

I know I am tired and run down. I hardly dare look in the mirror and for the lunch party I really couldn't be bothered to take any trouble but then I saw it was my duty to support my husband and if I appeared in this state he would think he and the doctor were certainly right to keep me from the baby. So I did my hair and changed into the skirt I bought on our last trip to London when Sophie and I had taken the afternoon off to go shopping together – and after this things seemed better, although I knew that my eyes must seem dull and exhausted, no matter how much I pretended to smile. I heard the Cochrans' loud voices as I came out from the kitchen, both seeming so full of life and happiness or so pleased to be with us on this cold dull day and I thought – the only way to get through this is to talk to the one person and concentrate on them so that my mind is completely taken up either with listening to what they are saying or thinking of what I will say to them next that there will be no time to remember the rest of my life.

'You look marvellous.' John and Barbara Cochran said the same words as I came in. Rachel, the daughter, kissed me and said her first child was due in the summer. I saw she was already large, then they introduced her husband, a man called Stefan, and I remembered he was a foreigner, although I didn't think we had met before, and as Bob started talking again to the Cochrans about some plan he had to plant more trees on the hill that joins their property, I thought – I will talk to the foreigner because he is a stranger here and will be the one most likely to need help and may be happy to hear what I say.

I must describe him. Perhaps I can do this best by thinking of Bob, the man I have come to know best in the world. He is slightly shorter than Bob but not much – there can't be more than an inch or two between them – and broader, more thickset. Bob's hair is dark I know but this man's seems even darker because Bob's is more dark brown than black and people have told me that as a boy he was quite fair until the age of ten or eleven. It is not just Stefan's hair that is different but his whole colouring seems a strange mixture of the palest white of his skin – on his cheeks and forehead for instance – with the blackness of his eyebrows and eyes as dark as his hair which I know Bob will think is too long. I was sure those eyes were black and I must have stared at them because I noticed that he lowered his gaze in a shy way which made me feel slightly sorry for him.

Then he did look at me and I saw those eyes again with their strange darkness against the white around it – and it must have been this that made his stare seem so fierce that I had to exert my will to meet it. But the eyes did not burn into me in the way that Bob's do when he is angry – I could not have stood that from anyone else – they did not burn but they held me so that I did not want to move away from him and it is this strange feeling I remember as I write about it now.

He was dressed in a poorer way than the rest of us. His grey tweed jacket was too short in the arms and the sleeves ended far above his wrists, showing the light brown of what looked like an army shirt – although I noticed he wore a smart green tie. Although he was broader than Bob, the skin of his face and cheeks was tight over the bones and this, with the pale colouring, gave him a hungry look – or so I imagined it – and I thought the brightness in the dark eyes and his quick movements made him seem more alert and alive than the rest of us but when he answered me he spoke slowly in a voice not so deep as Bob's but still low, the words seeming to be held back as if he knew he must slow down.

'Rachel and I are living up here now.' I think it does me good to try to remember his own words, if only to use my memory. 'I like this part of England.' His English was clear and there was only the slight trace of an accent. I noticed he never shortens words or uses slang – and I said that it was now my home as well but I had no time to say anything else because I had to get them into the dining room before the food was spoilt.

The foreigner was beside me with John Cochran on my other side who spoke in that way he has – as if I was just a girl – so I told him about Charles and how lucky we were to have Beryl to help. 'Rachel refuses to have anyone,' John Cochran said. 'She wants to do it all herself. And Stefan is going to be called upon to take his turn with the nappies. Isn't that right, Stefan?' Stefan smiled at me. 'So I have been given to understand,' he answered. 'I hope I will be able to meet these new demands.' Rachel laughed at her husband and I thought – she is so happy, so in love. 'You're quite ready for it, my darling, aren't you?' she called out and said to me, 'He's most wonderfully useful, you know.' Then we were all looking at Stefan who smiled back at his wife and I thought I saw why the Cochrans were so proud of him and wanted us to see what sort of man their daughter had married – for John Cochran seemed unable to talk about anything else. 'Bob,' he said, 'you must show Stefan some of the new planting you've done on Weldon Hill. His family had forestry before the war, on their eastern estates. I'd like him to see the way woodlands are managed here.'

I knew that Bob did not like him. I could tell from the way his voice came out with that hard edge. 'Where was this?' he asked. Stefan said the names of one or two places. 'What's happened to the property now?' Bob asked. 'It has been taken over by the state,' Stefan said. 'Do you go back there?' Bob asked, his words coming more quickly but still with the same hardness. 'No. I am married and live here now.' 'Where?' 'With my parents-in-law at the moment.' 'What do you do?' 'He's helping me on the farm,' John Cochran answered. 'Why?' asked Bob. 'Because I need an extra man.' Bob turned back to Stefan. 'How did you get out of your country?' 'I was at Cambridge when the war began.' 'What did you do then?' 'I joined the British army.'

'See any fighting?' 'Yes.' 'Where?' 'In Europe.' 'What part?' 'When the war ended we were in the Rhineland.' 'Why?' 'Those were our orders.' Then Stefan said to me softly, 'Do you think I have passed the test?'

Then I laughed. I laughed and laughed and laughed and could not stop. I remember the way they all looked at me, trying to laugh too at first because they must have thought there was some joke they had missed — then through my own heaving and desperate attempts to get control of myself I saw John Cochran's worried face before Barbara stood up and came to me, putting her arm around my shoulder and trying to help me to my feet. Bob did not move. Yes, he even seemed at one moment to be looking away and before I stood up with Barbara and Rachel and Stefan, who was now at my other side, before I let them help me out of the room, I faced him and screamed — no word but a long scream as loud as I could manage through the end of the laughter — and he turned his head as if hit at last.

They took me to the drawing room and when I was on the sofa I found I could talk because the laughing had stopped and the fear as well. Barbara Cochran sat beside me with Rachel on the other side, Stefan standing some distance away and I could see Bob and John come into the room. I heard Bob say, 'She's all right. The doctor told me to expect this' — and I wondered if he thought he was speaking quietly or was not even trying to keep me from hearing these cold, harsh words. 'Would you like to be left for a bit?' Barbara Cochran asked. 'Let me put some more wood on the fire. Stefan — perhaps you could do it?' — and he moved towards the basket of logs. 'No, no,' I answered, 'we must finish lunch. There's a pudding. I'll get it out of the oven. Please, let's go back to the dining room.' I stood up, wiping my eyes with a handkerchief. Bob did not come to me but seemed to move backwards, towards the wall in order to be out of my way when I came into the passage. 'I must go down to the kitchen,' I said and turned off towards the pantry and the stone steps that lead to the basement and they seemed to be trying to stop me, so I walked quickly away from them, almost running into the pantry and hearing my feet clatter on the stone as I rushed down the steps, turning round at the end to see that no one had followed me after all.

I found Beryl sitting at the great long wooden kitchen table. Quickly she stood up. 'Is there anything the matter, Mrs Layburn?' – and all I could think of was to ask her what she had done with the baby. 'He's fast asleep upstairs.' She watched me and again I felt I must say something to her to let her see I was not ill so that she would not have an even better excuse for getting together with Bob and refusing to allow me to see or touch my child. I started to complain about the oven as I opened its door. 'I don't think the boy fills the stove up with coke often enough,' I said. 'Will you remind me to say something to him? It should be hotter than this' – and she answered that she had not noticed any difference to the way it had always been as long as she'd worked here.

When I brought the dish into the dining room, the talk stopped and they all looked at me. Barbara Cochran came across to the sideboard. 'My dear ...' she began, but I interrupted and called out that everyone should come and help themselves and they did what I wanted, the men coming last, Bob saying nothing to me at all. When I sat down again at the table, John Cochran said, 'You've had a hard time of it. Bob was telling me' – and Barbara leaned across to say, 'You must rest now, Catherine. Plenty of rest – that's the best cure. Bob tells me you've got this marvellous girl to help,' and then Bob did speak to say, 'Dr Maltby comes again tomorrow.'

I don't know why I turned to him first. You might think I would choose John Cochran because he is probably the person that Bob and I have seen most of since we married and came to live up here together. Like Philip, like almost everyone, he has said to me again and again how happy Bob looks. But something kept me from him at that moment, partly the way he never treats me as a grown-up, always as a girl, also I suppose because Bob and he are close – or as close as a person can be to Bob – and I wanted to be free for a moment so as to keep my mind from suddenly breaking again. I did not even think Stefan might feel awkward with me – no, I just asked him about his life as if nothing had happened, without even the sign of a crack in my voice which made me feel quite proud at last.

He spoke slowly. He was a refugee, he said. Most of his family had died in the war although he had a sister who lived in America and a brother in Paris with his mother and father. Some of his cousins had stayed on. He did not envy them. He would not like to go back, especially now that he had Rachel and this new life with her family in this part of England. His father-in-law had given them one of the farmhouses. They hoped to move into it some time next year, when the builders had finished and their child was old enough to give Rachel time to arrange the place how she wanted. 'I have been lucky,' he said. How much better it all was than the flat off the Brompton Road where they were living a month ago. 'I learned about trees as a child,' he said. 'That was what I was going to do if there had been no war – learn English at Cambridge and then go back to our forests in the east. Will your husband show me his woods?'

Bob might have heard my answer – but I could not help it. 'I can take you,' I said, then quickly again, 'Let me take you.' At first he seemed surprised. Then a look of wonder came on to his face – only for a second I swear, but I saw it and I knew he must know what was really happening to me behind the scene that had just taken place because he could understand even more than Philip and I was certain of this in that one moment. That was all. After lunch they left. Bob said to me, 'You must rest,' and I was relieved he did not refer to the way I had broken down except to say, 'Why did you laugh like that?' and I answered that I was tired, which seemed to satisfy him because he knew the doctor was coming tomorrow and he could go back to that world of his own. Then I went upstairs and started to write which is what I have been doing all this time.

Four days have passed. I can count them off. I can count them with this extraordinary feeling inside me because I have been saved.

Dr Maltby talked to Bob. I don't know what he said but Bob started to pay more attention to me. The night after the doctor's visit he reached out to hold my wrist in bed and asked, 'Are you all right?' and I thought – after all these months he is going to try to make love now but I do not want it, so please don't and the hand moved as he turned away as if in answer to my wish. The next morning he told me that John Cochran had telephoned to ask if Stefan could see the woods. 'I have a meeting,' he said and smiled and then I felt strong enough to say, 'Why don't I take him? The doctor said I ought to start going out more now in this good weather' – and it was true that Dr Maltby had suggested I should go for walks by the sea in this strange sun of an early spring, even though we are still in March. Bob said nothing at first. I waited. Then at last he asked me if I knew where to go and explained exactly where the trees were. I could not stop myself saying more. 'I could take Stefan down to the beach as well. It's only a short drive from the wood and Dr Maltby said I ought to try to get some sea air,' I said and he told me to take care.

Oh, Philip. I did think of you. I thought of you and how we had come so close yet were always separated by these last barriers – the distance we are forced to be from each other, the way there is always the feeling that our friendship is haunted by your secrets and my secrets which neither of us will ever quite give away. That was the trouble last summer – and now it seems better almost to write than to meet, something I would never have imagined a week ago. I know what you have taught me, what your mind has done – and this should be much more than anything that happened yesterday by the sea. I will not dare tell you in a letter but I will write it here and hope that perhaps one day you may see and understand. Because the woods were wonderful in the sunlight and afterwards we drove to the beach and walked together and it was here that Stefan spoke to me about his childhood.

'I remember the rafts on their way down the river,' he said. 'Those great logs, lashed together to be floated down to the mills. The raftsmen would build huts – small huts – at one end of the raft where they lived on their journey. Once, walking with my father and his dogs, I saw three of these monsters – great monsters of the river, gliding through the water. It was almost dark. In each hut a fire had been lit and glowed across the field. We walked closer to the river bank. Perhaps my father thought I would be interested. The night was still – the only sounds the cry of a bird, the rustle of our footsteps, the river, the knocking of timbers as a raft collided gently with the one ahead. It was spring, so the snow had melted. You can't imagine what those springs were like, for they don't exist here. Would you believe it when I say that the earth used almost to explode with life? Then there were those rafts on the clear evenings that spoke to me, even at that age, of the summer to come. My father called out to the men, two or three of whom were standing on the logs. They answered, waved their hats at him, then were gone as their monstrous transports rounded the corner of the river. One of the men was singing – well might he sing in that wonderful light! – and his voice stayed in the air, dying slowly after the rafts had disappeared. My father called to the dogs. We walked on. I don't think I was conscious then of a particular feeling of happiness. At that age – and I was very young – one accepts most things. Only now, in one's memory, do they rise up again like dreams, not quite real in this new world ...'

'Have your parents been here?' I asked.

'Oh, yes.' He looked out to sea, the flesh pale on his gaunt face, and his hair was lifted suddenly by the wind and I saw grey amongst the black, yet he cannot be more than thirty. 'They are happy for me, my parents. My father has this idea of England from his time in London before the First War – riding in the park, dances at the great houses of the nobility, the young men on leave from Oxford or Cambridge, falling in love one summer. He thinks also that I will be free.' Then I felt the first of the rain – one drop and another and another until it became a downpour and he put one hand on the sleeve of my old brown coat. 'We must take shelter' – so we ran to that row of old huts beside the embankment and the first hut was locked and the second and the third, then one of the doors opened at last. The floorboards had holes in them through which I could see the fine white sand but enough of the roof had survived to protect us from the rain.

It was dark in the hut. The windows were boarded up with strips of new wood and the only light came through the open door and a long crack in the wall. We sat on a bench at the back. The air was warm and stale. 'Are these places used?' he asked. I told him how tramps and gypsies sometimes came here but the huts were in a bad state and Bob thought they should be destroyed. 'But they are charming,' he said, 'even in the rain, in this state of decay. You must not let him.' He looked straight ahead, towards the half-open door and the beach and the sea in the distance where the tide was out across the sands. 'Catherine,' he said, 'you are not happy. Why? Will you let me help you? I can't keep away from your beauty. Please forgive me, Catherine' – and he turned to put an arm across my shoulders. 'Aren't you cold?'

CHAPTER TWELVE

T HE SOUND OF FOOTSTEPS, THEN THAT KNOCK AT THE door.

'Come in!' George shouts.

Again it is Bligh.

'I say, I hope I haven't come back too soon. But the light is going and you said you might come out with me. Don't let me press you.'

'I would like a walk.'

'Oh, good. Well, come down to the hall. I'll wait while you put on more clothes.'

It is cold outside. They walk towards a gate and the grass of the park, planted with ancient trees that are indistinct through a light mist. 'I have the key,' Bligh says and they pass through the gate, the older man keeping a slow but steady pace.

'The woman in the portrait...'

'Which woman?' Bligh turns to him. 'You mean Catherine?'

'Yes. Why did she die so young?'

'A rare disease. Something to do with the blood.'

'She must have been rather beautiful.'

'Rather beautiful?' Bligh laughs. 'What a curious way to describe someone. Rather beautiful. Not beautiful but rather beautiful.' He laughs, then stops. 'I'm sorry. I don't know why I should find that funny. Yes.' He walks on for a few paces. Now a low hill looms to their right. 'Well, you've seen the picture. My dear boy, how can I describe her?' He seems to stumble, almost to lose his balance, then recovers.

'Do her children have that look?'

'No, not really. Charles will be here tonight, probably late. He drives up from Catterick Camp.'

'And the other one?'

'Damian?'

'What about him? Has he more of her?'

'Perhaps. Yes – in the cast of his face, those large solemn eyes, the long lashes, the gentleness. But Damian has something of Bob as well: that mixture of awkwardness and elegance. One never sees him now. The last thing I heard was that he had decided to go to Madras to study at some academy of Indian music. He was always musical, even as a small boy. Catherine used to get someone to come up to the house to give them both lessons: Charles and Damian. I remember it well – those two small boys playing duets together in the drawing room, the sound of crashing chords echoing all over the house, for children rarely play with much finesse. One year I came for Christmas and we sang round the piano: "Silent Night", "O Come All Ye Faithful", "The First Noel".'

'Were they happy together?' The words come in a rush.

'You mean the family?'

'No, the Layburns.' He calls them by their Christian names for the first time. 'Bob and Catherine.'

The silence lasts long enough for him to wonder if Bligh has heard the question, then to fear that he may have entered forbidden territory. Perhaps he should apologise and ask quickly about the house, the park, the pictures, the likely state of the roads for his return journey tomorrow. Then at last, as they approach the first small hill, Bligh speaks. 'Inevitably there were tensions.'

'Yes.'

'I knew them both well.' He brushes his hand over his

forehead. 'In the beginning, of course, I was Bob's friend. Then he married Catherine and they came to live up here. I stayed with them from time to time and, given the fact that she and I shared the same interests, we soon found ourselves talking easily to one another. You see, she wanted to hear about what was going on in London: the theatres, concerts, exhibitions, that sort of thing. Perhaps, in a small way, I could bring these things alive for her. I'll never forget, for instance – on one of their trips south, soon after they had married, Bob was busy one morning, seeing lawyers about something or other, and I took Catherine to one of those lunchtime concerts at the Institute that old Geoffrey Kirk used to put on. It was a string quartet and they played some Schubert – the D Minor, I think. In those days the two Rembrandts hung on the wall opposite the door in the main gallery: the self-portrait and the one of the old man. I believe they've since been moved, probably rightly – but they contributed to the sense of occasion at those concerts. Catherine wanted to know all about them and the history of the collection and the Schubert – the Institute, the pictures, the artists, the music. When the quartet started to play I had to stop her, otherwise she would have gone on with her questions.' Bligh pauses. He seems to catch his breath and his voice sounds strange when it comes again. 'Afterwards we had lunch. She was to meet Bob later that afternoon. Then they were to travel north. Their first child was expected in the autumn – and their next visit south was not to be for some time.'

'They must have been often alone together up here.'

'Oh, they were.'

'But presumably there were other people. Neighbours.'

'Ah, yes. Catherine told me about them.'

'Who were these people?' Then he tells a lie. 'You see as a child I used to come up for holidays to the coast, with my parents. We had relations here, on the coast. They've moved now ... My father would bring us north for the summer holidays. It seems strange, doesn't it – to go north in search of the sun?' He laughs. 'But we met some people. My father had connections with the farming community. He did some dealing in agricultural machinery, you see. For instance, there were the Cochrans, I remember. An old man, a retired colonel, I think. They would ask us to have lunch with them.' He laughs again and feels better after these lies. 'I remember how pleased I was to get away for an afternoon.'

'Cochran?' Bligh repeats the name. Of course, 'Cochran.' He says the name again. 'Did he have a daughter called...?' Bligh's memory falters.

'Rachel.'

'That's right. She married a foreigner, a man from Eastern Europe.' Bligh feels a warmth in his cheeks in spite of the cold. 'Stefan.'

'I never met her,' George hastens to say. 'But Colonel Cochran used to speak often of the Layburn family. He admired Catherine.'

'And Bob?'

'I can't remember.'

'Rachel.' Now Bligh is sure of the name. 'She went to live in London. They came up for a short time, Stefan and she, when he was out of a job. Then they went back to London.'

'Stefan was the husband.'

'Yes. The foreigner.'

'What did they do here?'

Bligh stops and looks back at the house. 'If we go round by this clump of trees, there's a path that takes us to the other gate that leads into the garden.' The light is fading. 'I'm sorry. You were saying?'

'What did Stefan and the daughter do up here when they lived with her father?'

'Didn't the Colonel tell you?'

Bligh is tired. He wants to go back. Now it is almost always the same. He starts on a book, a walk, a conversation –

and then he gets tired, in spite of his interest. Poor Catherine. All these questions. He remembers their walks together when she had wanted to know so much and had seemed to be in such a hurry, in such a desperate state. He had begun gradually to see the truth of her loneliness. He had come to know on their walks together when he might expect more revelations by the tone of her voice, by the lowering of its note and the look of embarrassment and guilt on her face; then he had scarcely been able to hide his excitement. It was as if her beauty, his old feelings for Bob, the history and the strength of the place itself had come together to fool him, to make him imagine that he might be in love. Such thoughts had shocked Bligh. No, he had told himself: we are friends, Catherine and I. I want to help her, to be of use; that is why I go on these long walks across the park and into the woods and sit for hours beside her in the drawing room while Bob is out at a county council meeting or in search of some animal or bird that has been seen nearby.

Then suddenly it had ended, that part of his world. He should have been alert to these early signs in her letters when, soon after the birth of her first child, the Cochrans had come to lunch at Cragham with their daughter Rachel and her husband Stefan (Catherine had not caught his other name). Stefan had been put next to her, she had written. He seemed strange, rather wild – or so Catherine had thought – and that was all: none of the meandering descriptions and theories with which she had usually filled her letters, using words with that profligacy which Bligh had seen as a symptom of a sad and frustrated life.

'No.'

Bligh hears that George has answered his question.

'I'm not sure,' he says. Then he remembers. 'That's right. The man had been looking for a job in London but could find nothing. They had no money, you see. No money and no home. There was a child on the way.' Now it is all rushing back to him and his words come more quickly, then faster, as if he is frightened that the memories may go. 'They had had trouble with their landlord. Somewhere off the Brompton Road. My God, yes! Stefan couldn't get a job. So her father said – look, why not come up here, for the rest of the winter at least? Stefan can help on the farm. We need an extra pair of hands.' Now he is quoting Catherine's words, repeating almost exactly the conversation he and she had had on his visit to Cragham that distant summer.

He should have guessed from her letters. Had she tried to tell him? Bligh thinks: damn this youth, the boy in the crowd. How could he hope to understand? Young people today ... They look at things differently. Then we seemed to have time to talk about the concerts, the exhibitions, the parties, the changes that were taking place in a world that was slipping away from us both. Bligh had hoped that the friendship might have gone on forever: each feeding off the other, her solitude broken for a few days, he a fascinated observer of the drama and the pain. She and Bob: in the end (Bligh had thought) he would know everything. But that August, yes, surely he had been worried before his journey north because she had written less frequently and without those great outpourings of the past. He had not seen her for a year. Again it was hot.

Now Bligh recalls the beaten look of the trees, the grass tinged with brown, the sun faint in a clouded sky, the sensation of imminent thunder which would end the long drought. A taxi had brought him from the station. When he entered the hall, carrying his suitcase, he had found it all so precisely the same: the coats on the large round table, the boots and shoes around the tall hat stand, the heraldic creatures under the ceiling, the absurd stateliness of the portraits of the Viceroy and his wife, the bright tiles of the Mogul room. Even on such a warm day, there was a slight chill in the house. He had walked down the short passage into the drawing room where Catherine was standing by the fireplace, holding a book in one hand.

The light in the room had fooled Bligh, for she seemed to be wearing almost nothing as she came towards him, out of the sun, and in that brief moment he had felt charged with an astonishing burst of erotic power; yes, Catherine and he, here, now, in this room it would be possible and everything else in his life could be forgotten or changed. Then she came closer and he saw that she was wearing a thin pale dress that clung to her, that only her arms and the lower part of her legs were bare: these and her neck and the top of her chest down to where her breasts began. 'There you are.' She had kissed him but her words were between them: not the words so much as the cool way that she spoke, her eyes shying away, and his anxiety reared again, through the questions about his journey. In the past her greetings had been unguarded and usually after the first kiss she would hold the lower part of his arm or clasp his hand in a clear gesture of joy at the promise of two or three days' talk together.

'Bob is up at the farm. He'll be back soon.'

This had been wrong: for her to mention Bob at the start as if he, Bligh, was still Bob's friend. Surely these last two years had changed that and now it was Catherine whom he came to see: he who had been so close to her, who had heard her say things he was sure she had said to no one else. He had almost said, 'Look, please, is anything the matter? If so, tell me and we must put it right' – but it would have been useless, for the next day in the garden she had told him that she was seeing someone who seemed to know better than anyone else and of course he had not protested – for he could have no claims on her, no claims at all. But this new person: well. Her smile drew him on as they sat on the seat at the end of the lawn by the chestnut tree. 'I think I understand what love is,' she said. Then Bligh had excused his curiosity by thinking that he must try to help and make certain that Bob's marriage survived. Then there was the child: Bob and Catherine's child. No, he must keep her trust and this was why he had stayed with her on the seat, silent at first, then, as she seemed to want to change the subject, drawing her back with calm gentle questions. 'I can't speak about it. But I will tell you his name. He is called Stefan.' Her eyes had faced away, towards the house.

Bligh speaks aloud to George.

'Stefan, he was called, Stefan Trebinsky. I never met him. Never.' Now they are on their way back. 'They saw a bit of Bob and Catherine,' Bligh says. The thoughts, the memories, seem to have made his heart beat faster. 'The Trebinskys, that is.'

'Did you know the Cochrans well?'

'No.' Bligh's breathing is quick and he sees that he should slow down.

'My father told me there had been trouble. We used to see them every year. It was an annual occasion – our trip out to the Cochran farm.' Then George thinks: My God, what if there is a son or someone living there now? What if Bligh tells Layburn who rings up the son or whoever has the place? But he is leaving tomorrow for London, so there will scarcely be time for these two old men to find out that he has lied.

'Trouble?' Bligh asks.

'In the family. With the daughter's marriage.'

'Trebinsky was a shit,' Bligh says with vehemence.

'A shit?' The boy's voice shows surprise.

'Yes,' he answers. 'He took all he could get from the Cochrans.'

'The Colonel seemed upset,' George says.

'Upset? When?'

'On one of our visits.'

They have reached the house. Bligh pulls the gates closed after them.

'But you must have been a mere infant at the time,' he says. 'How can you remember what Colonel Cochran's feelings were?'

'No, no. We went there later.'

'Later than what?'

George blushes and stumbles over his words of explanation. 'Later than when I was an infant.' Does this make sense? 'It was my father who told me of Colonel Cochran's disappointment. Did the daughter and her husband stay long up here?'

Bligh knows the length of time, almost the precise dates. 'Just over a year. Then they moved back to London. He had managed to get a job. Then she had another child.'

'Colonel Cochran's daughter?'

'No. Catherine.'

She had come back to Bligh but not with the same sweetness and wish to confide.

At first he had feared that his visit to Cragham in August might be his last, for perhaps she had no further need of him. He had written a letter of thanks: a brief one this time, almost formal in tone, daring only at the end to refer to the 'excitement' of her new secret. An answer had come two or three days later, short again, about Bob and the weather and her opinion of a new book Bligh had told her to read: then, also near the end, the news that she had more to tell him but not in a letter and that he must come up again as soon as possible, and of course they would always be friends (he and she), no matter what happened.

So the exchange of letters had gone on. At first Bligh had thought: No, why should I, after what she has done? Then he had seen that there could be only a friendship (that weak word) between them: no love or ecstasy or the stuff of the dreams of the lonely or neglected. He must write back and say he will come north. He must suggest other books for her to read and describe some part of his London life. He was working hard, he said – and this was true, for he found comfort in his work, in those researches which had been his chief professional task since the visits to Italy at the end of the war.

Bligh looks back now over a great expanse of years – yet for her it must have seemed so much longer. He thinks he knows the length of her time with that man: a mere few months, a summer's romance – then the Trebinskys had moved unexpectedly south after the birth of their child, leaving the farmhouse for some work Stefan had arranged with the World Service. A mere few months: by the time Bligh had come north again, they had gone. He had watched for the tears that might come to her eyes, the moment of weakness. Then Bligh had had a new idea of romantic joy: not the beauty of Bob and her together but the fresh passionate affair with this stranger, a more adult liaison. How beautiful she had looked. Again it was the spring and her child was with her much more, running to her in the garden on a clear bright day.

'You look wonderful': again Bligh had said the words on the station platform for this time she had been there to meet him and her kiss was a proper embrace. 'I'm having another baby,' she whispered and then laughed and he wondered: What will she say to me now and who is the father – could it be him? She said only that the Trebinskys had gone south – and Bligh had looked at Bob and thought: Does he know? Because Bob had seemed different, not just withdrawn but melancholy through the stiff courtesy he showed to his guest and his wife. Once more he used the doctor against her. 'You must not sit out for too long, Catherine. Remember what Dr Maltby has told you,' he said and she obeyed but in a more self-contained way than before, as if these people and their customs meant less to her now because she had experienced a new love.

The rest can be flipped through, Bligh thinks: the torn pages of a calendar. The next child was born – the boy called Damian. Twice a year Bligh had come north to see Catherine and her children, that sweetness she had with them, and to hear her small difficulties: what was the best school for the boys? How could she persuade Bob that the upstairs passage needed repainting? Could Bligh try to make him see that something must be done about the books in the old library? Now Bob seemed to fit neatly into her life; she knew him so well, so completely. 'You know what Bob's like...' 'Of course I thought I could never get Bob to agree...' Once she had been so naïve, so sweet, so trusting, following Bligh's every hint or idea – but this had given way to a more precise coolness, as if he was still useful but essentially apart from the core of her life, the part that had been touched perhaps only by this man who had gone back to London with his wife and child.

'Are you happy?' she would ask Bligh from time to time – once (he remembers) the year he had spent Christmas at Cragham. 'In what way?' he had asked and she had mentioned Juan whom he had told her about all those years ago. No, he thought, that has passed: that stage when I could have said anything, almost anything – so he had answered – yes, I am more settled: and you? She had smiled: a creature of mystery. 'Oh, yes. Bob has his work and there are the children. It all turned out well in the end' – and no word of love or excitement or Stefan at all.

Did she see him again, Bligh wonders? As the children grew older, she took to coming to London more often. Always there had been the odd shopping trip or visit to her parents or sister, sometimes on her own, sometimes with Bob; now these came more regularly and usually she would allow Bligh to take her to a theatre or a concert or a function at the Institute where Geoffrey Kirk was in his prime. Occasionally, Bob came as well but it was Catherine who seemed now the more forceful of the two, her confidence matching her beauty; the looks of the two of them, Bob and she, shone out wherever they were. Was she seeing Stefan? Was she living two lives? If so, there seemed to be no sign of strain and it was Bob who seemed to be faltering as they entered middle age, his old friend Bob for whom Bligh began to feel sorry as he saw him so much alone at Cragham with his trees and his plants and his good work for the county: so much alone as she withdrew into herself.

Or had there been nothing behind Catherine's silence? Yes, Bligh thought, this was more pitiable – her entry into that dark tower, soon to be deserted even by her children when they grew up and left for the world outside. Then he had seen a dullness in her eyes, the odd flush as if from a spasm of heat. She said she was tired; perhaps it was the boys who were back for the holidays and seemed to need her so much. One night she had gone to bed early, leaving Bligh downstairs with Bob who had talked about some new tax that was going to hit him hard. Bligh remembers his angry words. 'Do they want to destroy us all, Philip? Is that it? What do those people in London think they're doing? Can you tell me?' At the end of the tirade, Bligh had asked about Catherine. 'She seems tired,' Bob had answered. 'It must be the boys. But what can you expect – a pair of healthy young lads like that? We both need a rest.' Why not take a holiday, Bligh had suggested, both of you together – when term starts again? Bob had looked at him: that sharp stare. 'Where would we go?' he had asked. 'I can't be away from here for more than a week. She knows that. No, it will be better when term begins. Then she can get to London for a few days. That's what she really enjoys. Will you keep an eye on her down there, Philip? I will be so grateful to you if you can' – and the stare had changed to a pleading look and it seemed as if his old friend might reach out to clasp Bligh's hand.

Bob had loved her, in his own way. So when Catherine had written from hospital, Bligh thought not only of her pain and anxiety but of Bob's as well. Then the doctors had sent her home but still she wrote of her tiredness, of how to be with the children exhausted her but she wanted to see that they had a good summer and Bob had promised to take them camping in the woods which was just the thing for the boys. Now Bligh knew that she was seriously ill. It was the length of time that made him see this, the days, then months that she had to stay in bed or be careful to do very little. She said often in her letters how she longed to see him – but he had not been able to get away, not even for two days, because of his work and this other boy: a different type this time, more intelligent than the others, a German called Franz. But how cold Franz had been: a machine, fascinating at first, then frightening, then repulsive. It chills Bligh to think of this heartless lust.

The telephone call from Beryl had brought him north at last. Catherine's face had no superfluous flesh; her hair, brushed back from her forehead by one of the nurses, hung limp around her head and those great brown eyes moved only with an effort. By the bed were some books he had advised her to read. She must have seen him glance at them for her first words after they had kissed were, 'You have taught me so much. Stay but not long because I must rest.' The nurse had smiled at him and nodded her head but had made no move to leave the room which was warm by the standards of the house; this heat had made Bligh realise that she was going to die. 'Are you working hard, Philip?' she had asked. 'The boys come from school to see me tomorrow. Isn't that nice?' He had told her that he hoped to come up again in the summer to finish the first two chapters of the great book that she had once said she was sure he had in him. Then she had murmured those strange words. 'Be kind to my friend if you see him. He means no harm. He doesn't know this country. Be kind to him. You are my best friend, Philip – my best friend' – and the nurse had pointed towards the door as he had moved closer to kiss Catherine goodbye.

Bligh had stayed the night. Those last words had rung out for him through Bob's talk at dinner about the estate and the children and her courage. 'Thank you for coming,'

Bob had said the next morning. 'It meant a lot to her. She's not too good today, so it would be better if you didn't go in to say goodbye. We'll keep in touch. Where will you be – in your London flat? Good. The gardener will run you to the station. He has to go in for a parcel. Don't worry' – and that had been Bligh's last glimpse of their married life before Bob's telephone call and the notice in the deaths column of *The Times*: 'Catherine, dearly beloved wife of Robert...' How typical of Bob, of the whole Layburn tradition, to use these stale ritual phrases to describe the uniqueness of one life.

Each person, each life, is an epic. This had been in Bligh's thoughts as he travelled up for the funeral. An epic of adventure, mystery and love – with heroes and villains and tragedies and triumphs. 'We'll keep in touch,' Bob had said again, still elegant, his voice rich with sorrow. 'I will expect you,' Bob had said and Bligh had obeyed, coming once, sometimes twice a year as he will come always now until either he or Bob dies as well.

'Who are those people?' George asks.

Bligh and he are on the lawn in front of the house and they see an elderly couple walking in the other direction, towards the drive that leads to the lodge and then to the road.

'They must be the tenants of one of the flats in the new wing,' Bligh answers.

'The new wing?'

'The Victorian part. Bob hides from them.'

'Hides from them?'

'Yes. When he sees them coming he hides behind a tree. He doesn't want to have to talk to them, you see.'

'Has he always been a solitary person?' George asks.

'Oh, yes. I think you could say that.'

'But Mrs Layburn . . .'

'Catherine?'

'Yes. I mean what sort of life did they lead up here? I know the Cochrans liked them.'

They have reached the front door and Bligh stands back to allow George to go through first. 'The portrait seems to have aroused your interest,' he says.

The boy blushes. 'Well, I used to hear about her from the Cochrans.'

'Don't worry.' Bligh laughs and puts his hand briefly on George's shoulder. 'It's only natural to be interested in a beautiful woman. Come, I'll show you something – if Bob is not there.' They walk into the gun room, which is now empty, and Bligh lifts one of the large, leather-bound photograph albums off the shelf. Here she is – or her life as she wished to preserve it, for she was the photographer, so there are not many pictures of her, except a few where she must have persuaded Bob or someone else to use the camera. George sees the family grow as the pages are turned, dogs and children on the grass in the summer sun, Bob standing with an axe beside a mutilated shrub, a picnic with Tony and Liz Blagden at the seaside, the boys on their ponies, then in the uniform of a well-known public school: apparently an ordered and happy progress through the years. 'There,' Bligh whispers and points to a photograph of her sitting on a seat in the garden, dressed in slacks and a dark jersey, laughing at the camera, one hand raised to push her hair away from the side of her head. 'See the simplicity. Will you go back to the old library now?' He closes the book and they both leave the room, to part in the hall.

On the stairs, just before he reaches the first floor, George sees the door of the old library open and Major Layburn come out, his face grim. He stops and their eyes meet.

'Have a good walk?' Layburn asks and strides briskly away down the passage, a dog quiet at his heels.

CHAPTER THIRTEEN

IN THE ROOM THERE IS NOTHING TO SHOW THAT
Layburn has been there.

George turns on the lights, looks at the Dutch picture on
the easel, then out at the darkening sky before he goes to
the small table and picks up the notebook from under the
cloth.

Oh, Philip, I saw him again – quite soon.

Bob had to go to London for three days on business
and I was left in the house with Beryl and Charles.
Stefan telephoned. I had written to him with no
thought about Rachel seeing the letter – I suppose this
new life of mine has made me daring at last. The
afternoon was the best time for him – so after lunch I
told Beryl I had to go into the town to the chemist. I
might be away for a few hours I said, because there were
one or two errands as well – nothing very important but
it seemed to be a good time to get these done before
the Major came back. She looked at me in that slow
way and I was frightened because now she knows me
so well. I smiled at her and said that Charles had been
out most of the morning with me in the garden so
perhaps she could keep an eye on him while I was away.
She leapt at this because of course she longs to have
him even more to herself.

The weather held. In the car I had to pull down the shield to keep the sun out of my eyes but there was a sharpness to the wind when I stepped on to the path that leads to the sea. Stefan was waiting in the hut. He had come early, he said, and had brought some blankets and what looked like an old green groundsheet. I must have looked nervous for he took one of my hands. 'Don't worry,' he said.

We sat on the blanket which covered the ground-sheet. I asked him where he had found all this, then wondered if I should waste time with such questions because we could have so few hours together. 'In one of the spare bedrooms,' he said and he laughed and I thought – what does he really think of us all? Would he much rather be back in his own country with his own people? 'Why are you free?' he asked. He drew me closer to him, his arm across my shoulders. The wind seemed to have dropped and the silence was broken only by the cry of a gull and then another bird as if in answer and I could not help thinking – if Bob were here he would identify these creatures, speaking their names aloud. The gull, the tern, the geese that fly in from northern Europe – how his mind races when he sees or hears them and I looked out of the half-closed door, wondering why I could not hear the waves and I saw the wet sand stretching away and the thin, shining strip of the withdrawn tide. Soon it must turn and start to creep in, stopping well short of us, although Bob had told me that two or three times in his life the sea had come up as far as the road, pressing on past the huts. Then suddenly I had an idea of Stefan and me, just the two of us, here, watching the water, clinging to each other as it came nearer and nearer until we were both swept away. 'Why are you free?' he said again.

I told him that Bob was away on business in London. Then I asked about Rachel because I was worried and he had not mentioned her name, so it was almost as if she was dead. 'She is with her mother in the house,' he answered. 'They know I like walking and they are happy for me to take the car in the afternoons to explore your countryside – so do not worry. We are safe.' He pulled me nearer to him so that our two bodies were touching but I moved away, for I did not want this man to think I was easy. He sighed. He was still close to me and with the sigh I felt his unhappiness – and we held each other and I knew suddenly that this was the last chance before we went back to our other lives.

'Stefan,' I said. Then he moved, first to my mouth with his mouth, then with his hands to pull up my skirt and press me down on to the blanket. I did not know what to do, so I thought – just wait, let him lead you in the way that the man should – for this will be different, different to Bob's roughness and neglect, for never before had I felt this strength flowing so fiercely across to me, out of him and into each small part of myself and Stefan was gentle as well as strong, so I knew he could make me do whatever he wanted, for he seemed to have beaten back all my old fears. This is life, this is the way I had hoped to live, even as he seems to become more anxious, in a greater hurry and takes his hands away and pulls at my clothes until I see that I must help and now my shirt is off, he pushes my jersey up, then my blouse, pulls at his own trousers, his breath coming in great gasps and I bury my hands into the blanket, grasping its folds and he enters and for a moment I feel we are completely together, yet I am his – no, this is not possible for he is pushing me off the edge of the blanket, then he finishes and says some words of his own language before patting my shoulder with his hand.

As we lay with each other afterwards, I heard the birds again, the gulls sometimes near, then far away ...

There is a knock at the door. George slips the notebook under the cloth.

'Come in!'

It is Beryl. As she stands there, he looks at her, remembering how much she must know, yet he sees only her well-meaning smile.

'The Major asked me to remind you that dinner will be at eight o'clock tonight,' she says. 'He was worried you might get so taken up with your work and forget. He thought you might be a bit confused about the timing of meals here after last night when they didn't eat until nine.'

'That was because I was late.'

'I don't think there's any criticism implied,' she replies and smiles again. 'It's just that the young Major will be here.'

The young Major? 'Is there another guest?'

'Major Charles. The Major's son. He's come up from Catterick for a couple of nights.'

Of course. 'Thank you.'

In the drawing room, a man is sitting on the sofa, reading a magazine. When George comes in, he gets quickly to his feet.

'Charles Layburn,' he says and walks forward with one hand outstretched: a tall man in his late thirties with dark brown, slightly curling short hair. His face has more flesh on it than his father's and is redder, coarser and fuller at the lips, without that mix of asceticism and elegance. His small eyes seem cool, his smile shown only by the baring of white regular teeth. His handshake is hard, almost painful. He wears a pair of grey trousers and a dark blue jersey over a light blue shirt which is open at the neck. In his hand he holds a glass. 'I hear you're up to look at the pictures,' he says. 'Can I get you a drink?' At the tray on the small table beside the piano, Charles Layburn pours out a glass of whisky. 'Where are you from?'

'London.'

They sit down beside each other on the sofa. Charles Layburn picks up a packet of cigarettes, offers it to George (who declines) before he lights one for himself in a fluent movement. As he blows the smoke out into the room, he settles back and looks up at the ceiling. 'Philip tells me that you work at a museum.' Philip? For a moment George cannot remember. 'Bligh.'

'Oh, yes. The Harman Institute.'

Charles Layburn smiles at the youth. 'Of course. I must go there when I have more time. The trouble with soldiering is that it take you to the most inconvenient places. Catterick, for instance. The only advantage is that I can get here quite easily for the weekend.'

His voice is higher than the old Major's, more nasal, and the words come out quicker, as if they might be uncomfortable within him. George searches for any sign of the woman in the portrait: no, Charles Layburn's eyes are too small, his face more florid, his nose flat because it has been broken. He remembers the photographs in the albums of the two boys: one of them both in shorts, another of Charles in long trousers and a tweed jacket, holding a gun, then the school boys in the black of their absurd uniform.

'Did you have a good journey?' he asks.

'Oh, yes. It doesn't take long.' Charles Layburn blows out more smoke. 'How did you get here? By train?' The eyes show impatience, perhaps dislike.

'No. I drove up yesterday.'

'Is that your blue van parked outside?'

'Yes.'

'I wondered whose it was.'

George Loftus tries a joke. 'I'm afraid it rather disgraces its surroundings,' he says and laughs.

'Why?'

'Well, it is rather ancient. Rather unkempt.'

'I should have thought that made it admirably suited to stand beside this house. Don't you agree?'

'Oh, but Cragham is magnificent.'

'You think so?' Charles Layburn stares at him. 'Perhaps you wouldn't be so keen if you saw the bills – or had to pay them.' At last he laughs. 'You're lucky not to be here in January or February. The heating system failed completely last year and we couldn't get it fixed until the end of March. It's the boiler, you see. It's so old that no one round here can cope with it, so we have to get someone out from Newcastle. Time ran out for places like these years ago – or that's what I think. No doubt you disagree.'

'Does your father . . .?'

'Does my father what?'

'Well, surely he is fond of the house.'

'Oh, absolutely. It's been his life really, hasn't it? Apart from the war I suppose.' Charles Layburn sips at his almost empty glass. 'Have you asked him? But perhaps you feel you can't. I understand.' He gets up and walks to the window. 'Look at the sunset. It should be clear tomorrow: fine enough to go out after pigeons.' Then he goes to the drinks tray to refill his glass and returns to the sofa. His movements are rapid, collected. 'What pictures are you working on?'

George mentions the Dutch landscape, the religious scene in the manner of Correggio and the two foxhounds.

'Oh, yes,' Charles Layburn says. 'Dad and I talked about those.'

'Then there's the portrait of Major Layburn's wife.'

'My mother? The one where she looks as if she's risen from the dead?' Charles Layburn laughs at his own joke. 'Good Heavens, I haven't seen that for years. It used to hang in the dining room when I was a child, over the chimney piece. Somebody put his foot through it. Isn't that right?

Quite a big hole from what I remember. What was the artist's name?'

'Burton. Oscar Burton.'

'He seems to have belonged to what one might call the necrophiliac school of painting.' Charles Layburn laughs. 'Corpses a speciality.' Then he feels he must explain. 'Oh, I know the fellow meant to capture her essence or whatever. But I can't believe it was necessary to be so morbid.'

'Do you think it's a good likeness?'

'A good likeness?' Some more smoke streams into the room. 'Not bad. But she did laugh sometimes, you know – and she was certainly very beautiful. The most beautiful woman I've ever seen. Can you believe that?'

At dinner, the old Major, Philip Bligh and George Loftus are in dark suits. The young Major, informal in his open-necked shirt, jersey and cravat, sits at one end of the table, opposite his father.

Bligh talks, fighting against the silence.

'What about a foreign posting?' he asks Charles. 'Something to take you away from the northern winter: perhaps to Hong Kong, the Gulf or somewhere east of Suez?'

Charles Layburn shakes his head. 'There aren't many places like that left now. The politicians have abandoned most of our old responsibilities. No doubt they were right to do so. One cannot swim against the tide of history.' He turns to George. 'Don't you agree?'

Bligh speaks again. 'What do you think, Bob?'

Layburn raises his eyebrows. 'About what?'

'Was it right for this country to withdraw from its old imperial outposts?'

'We had no choice. No use trying to turn the clock back, as Charles said.' Layburn's cheeks have a darker glow in the dim light. He gives George one of his sudden smiles. 'Wouldn't you say so?'

Bligh has not finished. 'But it means that there is much less scope for the young these days – or at any rate, for people like Charles here.' Bligh thinks that the young officer does not resemble Catherine at all, except in the intensity of his stare. He has no sensibility, no taste. 'We had a different burden: that of choice. When I was at school my parents tried to steer me towards the colonial service. It was thought to be an appropriate career for someone with my talents.' He laughs.

'But you chose art history instead,' Charles Layburn says.

'First came the war.'

'Oh, yes. So it did.'

'I had never seen myself as a lecturer or teacher.'

'Of course not.' Charles Layburn smiles.

'But I learned the job. I came to enjoy it.'

'Of course.'

'But you are teasing me.' Bligh turns towards George. 'Charles is the most frightful tease.'

'Have you finished?' Layburn asks suddenly. 'Charles, please help with the plates.'

With the next course in front of them, Bligh takes up the conversation once more. 'Bob, it really is the most extraordinary coincidence. You know, George was telling me that he used to visit the Cochrans as a child.'

'George?' The old man puts down his knife and fork.

'Loftus. Your guest.'

'Oh, yes. The Cochrans. They're all dead, of course.'

'Where did they live?' Charles Layburn asks. He could never have known them. After her death all contact would have been broken, for surely Bob must have found out.

'The other side of the moor, about ten or fifteen miles away. John Cochran had a farm. Quite a big place.' Layburn turns to his son. 'Where the Palmers are now. Fred and Betty

Palmer.' Then he looks at George. 'How did you meet them?'

He launches into the story that he told Bligh on their walk. His father's farming connections, their annual seaside holiday, the trips out to the farm . . . Then he leaps forward. 'Wasn't there a daughter?'

Bligh moves in his chair. 'I think . . .' he begins.

Layburn interrupts. 'Rachel,' he says. 'And she had a child. John left the property to them, you see, but they put it up for sale. Their hearts weren't in the place.'

'You have to be born here to appreciate this part of the world,' Charles Layburn says. 'That's why I'm surprised to hear of someone coming up year after year for a seaside holiday.' He looks coldly at George. 'Where did your parents live?'

George gives the name of the town. 'But my father had farming connections,' he repeats, then tells another lie. 'And my mother's aunt was married to a clergyman who retired to the coast, just a few miles from where we used to stay.' He relaxes. 'Then there were the Cochrans.'

'Fred and Betty Palmer have the house now,' Layburn repeats. 'The Cochrans sold up.'

'It was the daughter who sold the place,' Bligh says.

'And her husband,' George says.

'I can't remember these people at all,' Charles Layburn says.

'She married a foreigner,' his father says. 'What was his name?'

'Trebinsky,' George answers.

'Did you know them well?' the old man asks. Both Bligh and George search for signs of sadness, of regret, of recollected humiliation.

'No, no,' George answers. 'As I say, my father had farming connections. We used to drive out to their house. I was very young . . .'

'When did this man die?' Charles Layburn asks; 'I can't

remember him. I'm thirty-eight.' He looks at George. 'How old are you?'

Of course, the sums do not add up or subtract or whatever. George adds three years to his age, a mere gesture. 'Twenty-six.'

'John Cochran went years ago,' Layburn mutters. 'Then his wife moved away. The daughter and son-in-law thought of letting the place, from what I remember. Then they sold it. He worked in London. Trebinsky – that was his name.'

Charles Layburn speaks slowly so that no one should miss any of his words. He has a passion for detail. 'Now wait a minute. The Palmers have been there for as long as I can remember. I used to go to the parties they gave for their son Desmond, the one who works as a solicitor in Manchester. Then there was the daughter Sarah. She went to America and never came back.' All the time his eyes are on George. 'How old did you say you are?'

'Twenty-six.'

'That's twelve years younger than I am. I don't see how you could have ...'

Bligh breaks in. 'What happened to Mrs Cochran, Bob?' he asks.

'Oh, she died, years ago. As I said she moved away. She didn't survive old John for long. Probably all for the best.' The old man looks out into the room, away from his guests and his son. 'I don't know what happened to Rachel, the daughter. He's still around. Trebinsky. In London. Sometimes I hear from him. Letters, messages, that sort of thing.'

'What sort of thing, Bob?' Bligh asks.

'Nothing much. Shall we go next door?'

No one dares to mention that name for the rest of the evening and Bligh moves the conversation on to Charles Layburn's time in Northern Ireland where he and his regiment served eight or nine months ago, to stories of border incidents, careful analyses of the Irish character and a longish lecture on the importance of learning the lessons of history.

CHAPTER FOURTEEN

GEORGE HAS TAKEN THE NOTEBOOK TO HIS ROOM. IN bed, wearing a jersey, for the air is still cold, he opens it and finds the place quickly.

'As we lay with each other afterwards, I heard the birds again, the gulls sometimes near, then far away ...'

Wait.

He puts the book down. What has happened? Every night for the past eight or nine months Pat has been in his thoughts: Pat with her red hair, her stare of provocation, her slow words that draw him on, the girl of those desperate dreams. How often he has wished to know more about love and the beauty it can bring to two young lives – for there is no beauty in his thoughts of Pat, not even the sad, twilight beauty of Mrs Kirk's remembered past or his mother's memory of those flowers in a municipal park. 'And such marigolds ...' This is all he has wanted, all his life, from his earliest days in his parents' home to these lustful imaginings: a place where the soul and his desires may meet, where love rises out of the ruins of a thwarted life like this beautiful girl on the seashore beckoning to him across the years so that they may go into the hut and make love and she will speak honestly of her fears and troubles and he will comfort her, the two of them together at last, he and this fugitive from the immortal past.

★

As we lay with each other afterwards, I heard the birds again, the gulls sometimes near, then far away. Stefan held me. He seemed to sleep for a bit and I thought to myself – this is better, if he sleeps he will not feel too guilty but the sleep did not last, for soon I felt his hand grip my shoulder. 'We cannot be away for too long.' Then he drew me to him. 'But why not?'

We made love again, this time more slowly and I seemed to feel his excitement in his own pleasure, for we were alone with each other then, away from the hut, the blanket on which we lay, the sand into which I buried my hands, the sounds of the birds, the whole world outside. This must be love, I thought, and at the end I almost wept as I heard him say when he lay beside me once more, 'I know that I love you now.' Then I saw that he was crying and I could think of nothing except to ask if we should leave this place separately so as not to be found out. 'No!' Stefan hit the ground with one of his fists. 'Why should we hide the truth?' He dashed one hand across his forehead and a lock of hair fell forward on to his thick eyebrows. 'You are right,' he said. 'Do you want to go first? They're not expecting me back until late. They think these walks of mine are a sort of madness.' He held me and I thought – no, surely he can't want to have more. Then his grip relaxed. 'Is this mad?' I looked out of the door towards the sands and the sea where the sun had disappeared. 'Are you not frightened?' He smiled and traced a line down my cheek to the corner of my mouth. 'We may be at risk.' He wanted to see me again. 'What about tomorrow? Here?' I was brave and said – no. Come to Cragham at the same time. Bob is away – and he looked surprised and I thought I saw the love in his eyes.

That evening I did everything more slowly. I walked more slowly into the house, took the stairs one by one so that I climbed them at a slow speed. I did not rush as I usually do but I was pleased to see Charles and Beryl kneeling on the floor amongst the toys and the way they smiled at me. Beryl stayed on her knees and said, 'We were wondering ...' Then I spoke quickly. 'Oh, I went on a walk and must have taken a wrong turning in the woods.' Then I lied again. 'Major Layburn wanted the dogs to be given a proper run every afternoon while he was away.' Beryl stared and I thought – she is slightly simple and cannot possibly know or guess what is going on. 'But the dogs are still downstairs,' she said. 'They've been in all afternoon. They were there when we went into the garden and when we came back again.'

I started to talk to Charles who had some story of how he had lost one of his new shoes but I could feel myself blush. 'Is it too cold up here for you, Beryl?' I asked to show that I care for her. 'Cold?' She looked surprised. 'It's no worse than yesterday.' I went on, 'I mean, I was wondering if I should ask the Major if we could put another of those paraffin heaters in the passage.' She smiled. How she adores Bob. 'Oh, I wouldn't bother him,' she said. 'We come through the passage quickly enough, don't we, Charles?' 'Beryl,' I began. Her eyes seemed to get smaller behind her glasses. 'Yes?' 'Beryl, I have an appointment tomorrow afternoon.' Then I lied again. 'A man is coming to see me about insurance. At three o'clock. Could you take Charles for a walk at the same time as you did today? You know the Major and I feel he should have as much fresh air as possible.' She looked at me as if she knew it all. 'Would you like us to take the dogs as well?' she asked. 'Otherwise they won't get out all day.'

But I felt strong enough for her. Let her say or think what she likes because my courage has come at last and that evening I was pleased with myself and smiled at Beryl and Charles as if they could do nothing wrong, for I wanted to get Stefan to Cragham to show that I was not frightened, to show I was prepared to take risks for the first time in my life. This was something I had learned from what Philip had said – how we must search for beauty and freedom but poor Philip made me think also of frustration, of beating my head against stone, of how I had always held back a part of me and it was partly Philip's life and unhappiness that made me so daring and not think too much or worry or hide or lose my last chance so on that afternoon I could hardly wait to hear the sound of Stefan's car.

At first I thought of sitting in the hall, well, not sitting, for that would look strange to Beryl and also to him when he arrived and I wanted our meeting to be so natural, but then I could not help myself and did go down, five minutes before he was due. To begin with I stood by the hatstand, pretending to search through the hats and coats that were hanging there, then moved to the round table and the large bowl with the secateurs, keys, balls of string, cartridges and a small pair of binoculars, mostly things to do with Bob's work in the garden and the woods. I started to look at these, turning them over one by one, trying to identify the keys, holding the binoculars up so that I could focus the lenses for I knew I must not be too impatient at such an extraordinary and wonderful moment. Then I heard a shout from outside and went to the window. Surely not. No, it was a woman's voice and there were Charles and Beryl walking away from the house towards the gate that leads into the park, with the two dogs running ahead of them. They would not be out for long, I knew, because Charles would get tired and start to complain and there was the tea to prepare. I knew the routine so well from the hundreds of times I had lived through it but I did not want them to see Stefan and as I was thinking this his car came up, the front door opened and he was with me, wearing a dark blue jersey and a shirt open at the neck, kissing me on the forehead, those fierce eyes bright under the thick eyebrows. A man who had come about the insurance – to look at him anyone could see that this was ridiculous especially when he ran his hand through my hair and whispered, 'Where shall we go?' We walked out on to the lawn. Charles and Beryl were the other side of the park gate with their backs to us, still walking slowly away from the house – then Charles turned, looked straight towards us, waved and said something to Beryl who turned her head to see me wave as well. 'They have seen us,' Stefan said and I told him I had the excuse that he was the man from the insurance company, here on business.

It was not until we had reached the small summer house at the end of the walled garden that I noticed he was carrying a large canvas bag. He must have seen me looking at it for he said, 'The grass is damp. And I thought we could not go into the house. So I have brought some protection.' He opened the bag and took out a large tartan rug which he laid on the ground.

First we sat down and then lay together. 'I no longer think of going home,' he said. 'For this is where I want to be now above everywhere else. Here. Moments still come back to me – a scent in the air, the sharpness of those first winter frosts, the sound of horses on cobblestones, the glow cast by oil lamps in the evening, so much more gentle than the electric light. Do you know that rather than give all that up a cousin of mine shot himself – when the enemy arrived at his gates? He knew they were coming, of course, and he had made the preparations. People warned him. There were trains leaving and the roads were still open. But he was a bachelor who lived alone. He was old. His pleasures were over and he did not want to see this new world into which we have all been thrown.' Stefan looked up at the sky. 'Do you like me?' he asked suddenly and went on before I had time to answer. 'I know about your family – the history of the house, the man who went out to India, the commanders of the army. John has told me.' He smiled as I tried to say all this was not me but Bob and I am only on the edge, not a true part of it. 'You think so? And what am I?' Again he did not wait for me. 'Like you, someone on the edge. Tell me what has happened to you here, Catherine. Tell me the truth.'

At first I spoke slowly, choosing what or what not to say, but then the words came faster as if they felt free to leave me at last and I told him all of the story – or all I could fit into that sudden release of feeling and sadness – and he listened and then held me at last. 'It is over now,' he said. 'All that is over. Now we are together. This is all that matters.' But what about Rachel, I asked? He started to play with my hair. 'She knows me,' he answered and then began again what we had had in the hut by the sea. 'Please,' I said – because this time he seemed to try to move ahead faster, something I did not want. 'Stefan.' I called his name softly and I tried to push him off for he was already on top of me and over his shoulder I saw someone only a few yards away, staring at us through the break in the hedge. I must have cried out for he withdrew quickly and turned to see Beryl for himself.

She did not look shocked. Then she spoke. 'It's Charles. There's been an accident up at the house. I thought I must come and tell you. And the Major. He's come back.'

There is no more. George skims through the last pages of the book, finds them blank and puts it down.

CHAPTER FIFTEEN

H<small>E DOES NOT SLEEP WELL, PARTLY BECAUSE OF THE</small> cold. He gets up early, draws his curtains and thinks he must go back to the old library to see if there are any more notebooks. This morning he has to leave. It will take time to pack the pictures into his van. Then as he looks out on to the park he sees a man in white shorts and a brown jersey, running across the grass. It is Charles Layburn who raises his head towards the bedroom window. Although George knows that the young Major cannot see him from that distance, he steps back.

In the old library he searches the two cupboards and looks for other possible hiding places. The he hears footsteps and the door is opened. Again it is Charles Layburn.

'I saw the light on and wondered who could be in this part of the house so early in the morning.' He stands in his running clothes, short of breath, his hands on his hips, his face red and shining.

'It's seven o'clock.'

'Nobody goes into these rooms for months on end. I suppose that's why I was surprised to see the light. Interested in books as well, are you?' He looks at the cupboards which George has left open, then walks over to the easel, his hands still on his hips, and stares at the Dutch landscape. 'You're working on this?'

'Yes, I was just beginning . . .'

'Where does it come from?'

'It was painted by a Dutchman in the eighteenth century. The landscape is imaginary – based on what the artist remembered from a visit to Italy when he was young.'

'I mean, where in this house.' The young Major spaces his words, slightly baring his teeth as he speaks.

'I don't know.'

'I don't recognise the picture. But things are in such a mess here ...' He lets his words trail away. 'What else is there? I want to see.'

'Those ones up against the bookcase. I'll turn them round.' He walks across quickly and turns the pictures so that Charles Layburn is faced with the religious scene, the two dogs and the portrait of Catherine.

'The hounds used to hang in the bedroom passage. But what's this?' He came closer to the religious scene. 'It's in a dreadful mess. You're taking them all away with you, are you?' He points at the portrait. 'This as well? You know, it reminds me of my brother Damian. I've just realised that. Funny, isn't it? The thing has been hanging in this house for years and years and I missed the resemblance. He lives abroad, you know. In India. I heard from him the other day. He doesn't write often, so when one receives one of Damian's letters it's rather a special occasion. He told me he was about to go to Madras for the winter, to study music.' Charles Layburn laughs, an unnecessarily loud sound. 'What a mess.' He waves a hand to take in the room and its contents. 'Is it worth much?' Charles Layburn walks across to the cupboard beside the door. 'What do you think?' He takes out a bound copy of the *Annual Register* and the notebook.

'Why did your brother go to India?'

'Why do you want to know?'

He feels himself blushing. 'Just curiosity.'

Charles Layburn puts the books back in the cupboard. 'Damian is a sensitive soul. A caring person,' he says. 'He wanted something this country didn't seem able to provide for him – a belief, an idealism, call it what you will.' The words are clipped. 'I don't know what he gets up to now.' Charles Layburn stares at George. 'You find it all very exciting, don't you?'

'What?'

'The place. The pictures. The family and its history. Quite thrilling, really. Different, perhaps, to your own little life.'

'No.'

'Oh, so we're all the same, are we?' The young Major smiles and looks at his watch. 'You're not going till after breakfast, are you? Good. Then I won't say goodbye now.'

Bligh lies in bed as the light of the new day comes through a crack in the thick heavy curtains. He is not here but downstairs in the drawing room with Bob and they are talking about Catherine at last.

'She deserved more than I could give her,' Bob says. 'You knew that, Philip. You did your best to help. Even at the beginning, there were difficulties – those problems so many people of our generation seemed to have had because they did not know enough. But the two children were born and then you came to help us and you understood her far better than I could ever hope to do. You should have lived here with us, Philip, then everything would have been all right. You should have joined the family and written your book and Catherine might have helped in some way – with the research: you and she going round galleries together to look at pictures – then coming back to me and the children. What fun we could have had! You needed a home, Philip – with us to look after you, so there wouldn't have been all that nonsense in London with those boys. Isn't that true? And what happened? We were both pushed to one side – by another force which brought her the excitement and the happiness that neither of us seemed able to give or to know.

What was it? A physical force? Someone who could love and be alive in the way we have never been, in spite of all our ancestors and our courage and our reading and our sensibility? Who knows? But now we must stay together among the ruins of our lives. Don't you agree?'

He withdraws from this fantasy. Damn this boy Loftus, the face in the crowd: he has brought it all back with these memories of seaside holidays and trips to the Cochrans' farm.

As before, Bligh is alone at the breakfast table when George comes in.

'Your last day,' he says. 'Are you all loaded up? I leave tomorrow by train. At my age I don't like to face the motorways for more than an hour at a time. I was thinking ...' He waits for George to sit down. 'What a coincidence that you should have known the Cochrans. Bob was intrigued. You see, they were often here in the old days. Colonel Cochran's daughter Rachel was more or less the same age as Catherine, Bob's wife.'

'They came to live with her father, didn't they?'

'They?'

'Rachel and her husband.'

'Oh yes. Rachel and Stefan. Then they went back to London again. Catherine was sad to see them go.'

'Are they both dead?'

'I don't know about her.'

'And him?'

'Oh, I expect he goes on. Bob seems to have heard something. Didn't he say last night ...?'

The door opens. It is Bob Layburn, holding a newspaper.

'Good morning,' he says. 'Are you all loaded up?'

'Didn't you say last night that you'd heard from Rachel's husband?' Bligh asks.

'Rachel?' Layburn joins them at the table. 'Rachel who?'

'The Cochran girl.'

George watches closely but Layburn shows no signs of embarrassment. 'Do you mean the foreigner? Apparently he's connected with some magazine or newsletter, down in London. He seems to have put me on to his distribution list. In any case this thing arrives three or four times a year. He always said he was going to write. But I can't imagine why he sends me this stuff. Perhaps he thinks I'm a person of influence.' Layburn laughs.

'What is this magazine?' Bligh asks.

'How should I know? Most of it's in a foreign language!' Layburn laughs again. 'The language of his homeland, I suppose. There's a page or two in English. I haven't had time to study it in detail – but it seems to be for people like him who've had to leave the place.'

'Emigrés?' Bligh suggests.

'That's right. They have a world of their own, those people, don't they?'

'They can be great ones for conspiracy theories,' Bligh says. 'Plots and counterplots. Generally at the back of it all lies the vain hope of return.'

Layburn turns to George. 'But you say that you knew him?'

'No, no. My father had a connection with the Cochran family. A farming connection. I never met . . .' He searches for the name, only a moment ago so prominent in his mind.

Bligh helps. 'Stefan.'

'I'll show you a copy of the paper,' Layburn says.

Bligh interrupts. 'Bob, you never told me that you'd been sent this. After all, Stefan . . .'

Then Charles Layburn comes in and starts to speak.

'I thought I'd go to the far plantation this morning, to see if there are any pigeons about.'

In the hall, as George is saying goodbye to the three of

them, the Major hands him a newspaper. 'I found it in one of the drawers of my desk,' he says. 'I can't think why I kept the thing but since you know something of the family, you may be interested. Have a good journey.'

CHAPTER SIXTEEN

O N THE WAY SOUTH HE STOPS AT ONE OF THE MOTOR-
way service areas for petrol and takes the paper into the
cafeteria where, after buying a cup of coffee, he sits and starts
to read.

Most of it is in a foreign language but on the back page
he sees two or three columns in English under the heading
'News from around the World'. These tell of the proceedings
of a congress in Chicago and a meeting in Paris which had
ended with 'traditional folk dancing and singing of patriotic
songs'. There are several photographs in the paper, one of
the dancing in Paris, another of the crowded hall in Chicago.
Then, at the end of the last page, in small type, George sees
an address and telephone number. He knows what he must
do.

In the van he finds himself troubled by strange new
imaginings, strange because these are concerned with the
dead. So powerful are they that at times he is worried for
his own safety in the rain of the dull grey morning. Now
he is with Catherine, the melancholy dark woman of the
portrait, perhaps on the seashore with the waves in the
distance, walking together at first, then turning into the open
door of the hut where a blanket covers the sand as if it were
an invitation to lie there and rest before the two of them
begin to make love, their only witnesses the gulls and sea
birds whose cries echo above the sighs of delight and pleasure

he and she bring to each other; then the present comes back with the rush of the traffic and the spray thrown up by the great lorries on the journey south.

Now she speaks. 'George, will you help me? Listen to what I have to say. No one else knows this – no one – because there is not one person who can understand.' She tells him the story that she has kept previously for that soft-covered notebook and he takes her in his arms, listening to every word, even though he has read it before; then he asks gently at the end about the foreigner, the man who was married to John Cochran's daughter. 'Oh, that's over,' she says but still he must know more: did they meet in London after Stefan moved from the farm? He finds that this excites him: the thought of Catherine with another man, not only the awkward Major Layburn or poor Philip Bligh but someone who might show her the art of love. 'Yes,' she answers. 'We saw each other. Is that wrong with my life up here the way it was? Bob never knew, nor did Philip. No one suffered' – then she shows that it is time to move on and he sees in her movements and the way she takes the lead that Catherine is impatient. 'Look,' she whispers, 'follow me' – and his size and his reserve and his fears leave him as his mind fills with the thought of her, emptying only when he swerves quickly to avoid a car.

As he enters the hall of the house in Hampstead, Mrs Kirk shouts, 'George!'

She has been waiting. He is late because he had to take the pictures to the Institute first.

'George! Philip Bligh rang for you.'

'Can I use the telephone? I'll be with you in a moment.' He goes through to the small room that Geoffrey Kirk used as his study. He looks at his watch, sees it is half-past four and still office hours. He dials the number printed on the last page of the newspaper given to him by Layburn and it rings and rings; then someone picks up the receiver at last. 'May I speak to a Mr Trebinsky?'

'Who?' It is a man's gruff voice.

'Mr Stefan Trebinsky.'

'He is not here.'

'Is there some way I can reach him?'

'Please wait.' George hears the man speak quickly in a foreign language. Then the gruff voice returns. 'He has moved. Why do you want to speak with him?' The accent is harsh, roughening the words.

'I have an important message from his family.'

There is a pause. 'I have no telephone number. But I will give you an address.' The man reads out the name of the street. 'Number fourteen,' he says. 'It is south of the river, in Camberwell. As I told you, he has moved.'

'Thank you.'

'I do not think there is a telephone. Or not yet.'

George asks one more question. 'Is he still . . . ?' He searches for the right word.

'What?' The voice shows impatience.

'Is he still in good health?'

'In good health?' There is a grunt, followed by what sounds like a short attack of coughing. 'Yes, he is in good health.'

When he comes into her room, Mrs Kirk looks up from her chair with eyes that shine out of a pale, wrinkled face. He knows that she will want every detail of his trip, yet in talk so much can be spoiled, tarnished by dull phrases. 'How was your journey?' she asks.

He sits down on a sofa. 'Fine.' He tells her about Cragham: its shy owner, the sense of a world apart, what remains of a rich and vigorous past. 'It was cold,' he says and laughs.

'What about the pictures?'

He speaks of the large sporting scene in the drawing room – 'the best picture in the house' – and of the works he has brought back to the Institute. He mentions the religious scene, the hounds and the portrait of Catherine, 'the Major's wife'.

Mrs Kirk ignores this. For once she does not seem interested in the dead. 'What fun,' she says.

'The son was there last night. And Philip Bligh.'

'I know.' She smiles. 'He rang today, you know, after all those years, and left a telephone number. But it was you that he wanted. Did you ring him back from the study?'

'No. That was another call. Mr Bligh said he had known your husband. He said how much he had admired him.'

'Geoffrey?' She looks at the carpet and lifts a hand to her forehead. 'Did he?' She smiles again. 'Yes, Geoffrey liked Philip. They worked well together. So many people were in and out of the Institute in those days. We opened it up much more then, to raise money for the endowment fund, of course – but those occasions made the rooms come alive. After all, the place had been a home before it became a museum. Philip Bligh. He sounded just the same on the telephone.' She is quiet for a moment, then says, 'George, you won't forget to ring your mother, will you? Remember what we said. You should keep in touch with your family. Once a week ...'

The next morning, on his way to work on the Underground, George feels in his pocket to make sure that he still has the scrap of paper on which he has written Trebinsky's address. Throughout the day, during his report to Dr Friedrich, the examining of the pictures in the conservation department and lunch in the Institute's cafeteria, this is on his mind: so much so that he seems distracted and Friedrich wonders if there is something wrong with the boy.

'You saw the hunting scene?' the director asks.

'Yes. A magnificent picture.'

'It is famous, of course.' Friedrich's tone is that of a sneer. He has not much time for sporting art. 'What about the house?'

'Still standing but a little neglected,' George answers and thinks: What a dried-up man he is, like the shrivelled branch of a dead tree. 'Part of one wing is turned into flats.'

'What's wrong with that? More people should be living in these places. Surely that is better than a score of empty rooms.'

Then George realises that he has not seen or missed Pat or even glanced at the reception desk where she usually sits. Is she ill, away on holiday, dead? Is this freedom at last? No, it is merely the conquest of one obsession by another, he thinks that evening, as he turns his van away from Hampstead in the dark towards south London. He glances at the address on the scrap of paper on the seat beside him. The journey is not long but he feels as though he is taking part in some epic tale, as if the rest of the world must be watching. He waits at the traffic lights by Vauxhall Bridge, then drives on. From the bridge, the river shines like silk under the purple and black sky. He has looked up the directions on a map and remembers the names of the streets. Yes, Kennington, Camberwell, then to the left, then right and left again. The grey houses in the small crescent arch towards him. Above them, on either side, are the great towers of a new development, its insensible mass at odds even at night with the outdated elegance of the place where Stefan Trebinsky lives.

He stops in front of the house where there is an empty space, the only one in the crescent not filled by a parked car. For a moment he sits in the van and breathes once, twice, three times, then looks at the black front door. The door opens and a man is framed by it: a thin, tall man wearing a sheepskin jacket and a brown trilby hat. Could this be ...? He sees a small dog on a lead at the man's side: a dachshund, he thinks. No. He has not imagined Stefan Trebinsky as the owner of a dachshund. But he must not miss this chance, so he gets out of the van and walks to the steps that lead down from the house to the pavement. 'Excuse me.'

The man stares at him. They are face to face, almost touching each other. The dog barks twice, a sharp, high sound. 'Dinah!' The voice is English. There are no dark eyebrows or that disorderly hair, no trace of Stefan: only an angry look, a bald head and a mean, tight mouth.

'I'm looking for a Mr Trebinsky.'

'Who?' The dog barks again and the man jerks the lead.

'Mr Trebinsky. I believe he lives in this house.'

'There's no one here of that name.' The man scowls. 'The place is divided into flats. Has been for years.'

'But I believe he lives in one of the flats. A foreigner. He may have moved in quite recently.'

'Oh.' The look relents. 'Wait a minute. Somebody new has come here, to the third floor. To tell the truth I haven't spoken to him yet. Why you don't try the bell?' He points to the door, to one side of which there are four bells with small cards next to them. They peer at the words written on the cards. The top one is blank. The man pushes the bell and soon the small loudspeaker on its other side lets out a high-pitched hum. A voice calls through the noise. Is this him, this coarse, disembodied sound? No words, just a voice through a broken machine. Then, above the crackling, he hears the name Alfred.

'Why don't you go up?' The man says. 'The front door is open. I'll close it after you. It's the door on the left at the top of the stairs. Knock on it and he'll let you in or not as the case may be. Come on, Dinah. Good night.'

The stairs have a brown carpet and the walls are light green: a cold colour. He takes them quickly, two at a time, then knocks at the door on the top floor and it opens. George knows that this is him, this is Stefan. He sees the likeness, senses the man. Here in front of him is her lover and he looks still vigorous, his large presence thrusting forward; the head of thick grey hair still showing much of its original black, the alert face, the corners of the mouth turned down in high disdain, the searching look of a man on an unfinished journey. Then Trebinsky speaks.

'Where is Alfred?' The voice is deep, the accent still there.

'Mr Trebinsky . . .'

'Where is Alfred?' Now he is almost shouting. 'Are you the boy?'

'The boy?'

'Yes. Alfred's boy.'

'Mr Trebinsky, I've come because I wanted to bring you a message . . .'

Again he interrupts. 'A message? Here, let me look at you. Show me your face.' His large head comes closer to George who sees the grey and black stubble on his cheeks and chin and smells the staleness of his breath. 'No, it's all right.' These words are spoken softly, as if to himself. Then the voice rises once more. 'What message?'

'From Major Layburn.'

'From who?' An unbuttoned light brown cardigan hangs off his white shirt which is open at the neck. Heat comes through the open door.

'Major Layburn of Cragham.'

Trebinsky looks at the floor, then again into George's face with those dark eyes that had watched her. 'Well, you had better come in.'

The flat is bright with innumerable lamps and first he sees papers and books: books on shelves that take up the whole of one wall, on chairs and tables where there are also piles of paper and files. A cat leaps off a sofa, Trebinsky moves some of the papers and they sit down, George in the place where the cat has been and Trebinsky in a hard-backed chair which he moves out from a table. A gas fire set into a wooden chimney piece glows red, making the room uncomfortably hot. There is a smell of cats mixed with that of fried food. Then George notices a carved crucifix in one corner, the top of the cross touching the ceiling, its wood dark against the white-painted walls. 'I am expecting someone,' Trebinksy says. 'How can I help you? You say you are from Cragham?'

'No. But I've just returned from a visit there.'

'How is it?' He coughs and buries the lower part of his face in one hand.

'Still standing!' George tries to laugh but the other does not respond.

For a moment Trebinsky seems to talk to himself. 'That old barrack of a house.' Then he looks up and asks gently, 'How did you find this address?'

'I rang up the newspaper.'

'The newspaper? What newspaper?'

'The one that you sent to Major Layburn. It had a telephone number on the back page.'

'Oh, that. Yes, I had forgotten that I put him on our circulation list. They were looking for people of influence and I thought of Layburn. Does he have influence, you will probably ask? I will have to answer that he does not. But I wanted to give a small encouragement to the editorial committee. The address sounds grand, doesn't it?' He pauses, then coughs again. 'What is your message?'

George realises with a shock that he has thought of no cunning approach, no plausible excuse, having looked always beyond the dull preliminaries of the meeting to some great revelation. But he knows also that he must not stumble. 'That he wants to know more about the cause.'

'The cause?' Trebinsky leans forward as if he cannot hear.

'That your paper supports.'

'There is no cause.' Trebinsky laughs. 'Why has the good Major Layburn decided suddenly to take an interest in us? But wait a minute. Who are you? I know – you are one of those boys. What are they called – Charles and . . .? I forget. There were two children.'

'No, no.' George says his name in a rush of words. 'I went there to look at the pictures. You see, I work at the Harman Institute. Major Layburn wanted some restoration work done. He showed me several pictures and I brought three back to London with me. You may remember them.'

'I?' Trebinsky looks surprised. 'Why should I?'

'You lived up there for a short time.'

'That was years ago.'

'With your wife's parents.'

'My wife is away. My daughter lives in Australia with her husband and children and Rachel is on a visit there now. Last year I accompanied her. We have more time now that I have retired from the Corporation.'

'The Corporation?'

'The BBC. I worked for the World Service for over thirty years. Now what can I do to help?' Trebinsky's eyes are more kindly than he has expected. 'I do not want to hurry you but, as I said, I am expecting a visitor.'

'One of the pictures is of Major Layburn's wife, a portrait by an artist called Burton.'

'Ah yes. That poor woman!' Trebinsky shakes his head. 'I did not see the picture. But I heard about it. After I left that part of the world to come to London with my wife, Catherine wrote to me from time to time. She said that an artist was to paint her. She seemed to find the idea exciting. But that would have been in character.'

'Why?' He speaks quickly again. 'I have to work on this portrait and I thought you might be able to give me some idea of her.'

'But couldn't Major Layburn help?' Trebinsky pushes his thick hair back from his forehead and then brings his hands together, raising them slightly in the air. The only noise in the room is the low roar of the gas fire. 'Dear Bob. No, perhaps not. He was never the most forthcoming of men, although I came to admire him. You know about his war record? Also, he ran his property in the most conscientious way. I tried to get to know him when we were up there but he did not like me – not that he was ever discourteous. It may have been that old English distrust of the foreigner which was more evident then than now. After all, we are talking of nearly forty years ago. I was interested in the history of the house and the family – the generals and the man who ruled India – and I tried to ask Bob about that but he seemed to find it a terrible effort to have to tell me. I was sad because then I had a great passion for English history – not just your history but the country as well and here Bob was kind to me, for he allowed me to see his trees. I must have walked miles up there – on the moors and the hills, then down to the sea and those beaches. Do you know it well?' Trebinsky strikes the table gently with the palm of his hand. 'Now, what did you want?'

'Catherine Layburn.'

'Oh, yes.' Trebinsky frowns and looks briefly towards the great wall of books. 'Did you not meet her? No, of course. You are too young. Well, she was a dreamer in a charming way. Very beautiful. We were perhaps able to help one another. No, that is not true – because she could not have understood what it was to be as lost as I was at that time. She yearned for knowledge, for excitement as well. There was a man who used to come and stay with them whom I christened "the tutor" – some expert on art or paintings who could feed culture to her. But the excitement was missing. Bob was busy. There was a child but in a household of that kind arrangements were made to take him off Madam's hands.' He smiles at George. 'So Madam was left with a problem, that old problem – what to do?' He moves in his seat, then looks at the ceiling as if in search of more words. 'Look, I will tell you what I know. All this is in the cause of art, is that right? I believe you. You are a stranger but I believe you. Well, she was beautiful. Does the picture bring that out? If it does not, then it is not a good likeness. Yes, I should like to see the picture.' He looks at the surface of the table and smiles again. 'The tutor. What was his name? I never met him.'

'Philip Bligh,' George says.

'Philip Bligh.' Trebinsky's voice drops. 'She was pleased with Bligh. Bob was busy – too remote, I suppose, in the way that kind of Englishman can be. I am sure he did not mean to be unkind. The tutor told her to read all those books!' He laughs and has another short fit of coughing. 'I am sorry. Look, do you mind if I smoke?' He reaches across the table, grasps a packet of cigarettes and offers it to George before lighting up himself. With a sigh of pleasure he blows a trail of smoke into the overheated room. The smell mixes with that of the cats and the fried food. 'I ask because people are so hysterical about this habit now.' He points to the cigarette. 'The smallest intake and they assume it is the beginning of the end. But I have seen enough killing to know there are greater risks in life than the enjoyment of ten or fifteen of these a day. Now where were we?'

'Catherine.'

'Ah yes. Let me think – the child, the books, the visits of the tutor: she needed more than these. Now Bob Layburn was an admirable man – a man of honour, with a sense of duty and chivalry, those knightly virtues I came to respect.' Trebinsky stops talking and looks directly at George, his eyes cool. 'Don't you agree?'

'I wonder if they were suited.'

'Why?'

'I . . .'

Trebinsky does not press the point. 'There were some things missing. Even in the midst of all that, she did not have enough. True, there was a child – a boy. Now he must be grown up. What is his name?'

'Charles.'

'Yes. Charles. When you first arrived, I thought you might be him. Charles. Where is he now?'

'In the army.'

'They must be pleased. Bob must be pleased.' Trebinsky blows out more smoke and coughs again, putting his hand up to his mouth. 'Who did you say sent you here?'

'Major Layburn. Then I wanted to know . . .'

'Why did he send you?'

The lie is repeated. 'To ask about the newspaper that you send him.'

'There is nothing to tell. It is simply a newsletter for people from my country. An attempt to keep some sort of community together: a worldwide community. We have meetings, dances, congresses. It is mostly cultural, like the tutor. Not political, or hardly political – apart from the occasional display of hot-headedness. We do not promote futility.' He draws on his cigarette. 'How did you find me?' George tells of the address on the last page of the paper and his telephone call. Trebinsky nods, then says, 'How did you know that I had been friendly with her?'

'Major Layburn said so.' He decides he must take a risk. 'I wanted to know more about her because of the portrait. I have to work on it, you see. There seemed to be no one else who might know. Major Layburn did not seem to want to talk about her, perhaps because it upsets him. I didn't want to bring back painful memories.'

'What about this other man, Bligh? Have you seen him?'

'He's dead.' The words come out quickly, an instinctive response.

'So that leaves me. Why? Has she no family? The boy, for instance.'

'Boys. She has another son – who lives in India. They were too young. I wanted an objective assessment. Forgive me. I should probably not have come.' George makes as if to stand up.

'No.' Trebinsky shakes his head. 'Why not?' He shrugs his shoulders. 'Please. Don't worry. Catherine kept a journal she once said. I never saw it, of course – but the idea interested me. I found her curious – not unusual because I am sure there are many like her with that loneliness and romantic longing. Look at me!' Trebinsky raised his hands slightly. 'She seized on me – only in a way of speaking, of course. Let me try to be as truthful as I can. It was not one-sided, by any means. Think of this young man who thought he had found freedom, who was in love with the idea of England – the history and the country and that house which seemed such a fine show of this with those great ancestors: then her beauty and sadness to express it all for me. The Cochrans had been kind but of course the Layburn tradition was much stronger, much more intoxicating. I had read my Macaulay and Trevelyan and those other great story-tellers. But I wanted to hear it all from her – and in return I gave her my stories of loss and exile, the past I had left behind.' Trebinsky sits back. 'No, please, you must see. It was just romance: nothing more. A few walks and a few conversations. She had read too much. It was her tutor's fault: poor Bligh. How could he have known what he was doing to her? I was walking with a beautiful woman. That was all!'

George waits but Trebinsky has finished. 'In the portrait she looks sad,' he says. 'May I ask you one more question? Did her oldest child have an accident when he was young? Perhaps it was nothing serious. A broken arm or leg.'

'An accident? Not that I know of. Why? Does he walk with a limp?' Trebinsky starts to gather up some papers that are on the table. 'Now, what will you tell Bob Layburn?'

'Tell him?'

'About our paper. You understand that it is just an attempt to keep our community together?'

'Yes.'

'So tell him that.' Trebinsky looks at his watch. 'I do not want to hurry you but I am expecting a visitor. Will you give my regards to the Major?' He laughs. 'I doubt if he will want to come to see me down here. Now take care with the picture. You must try to bring it alive again. I felt sorry for her. That was all. Please be careful on the stairs. They are steeper than usual in these houses. I don't know why.'

CHAPTER SEVENTEEN

HE DRIVES ACROSS THE RIVER, THROUGH THE WEST End, up towards Swiss Cottage, to the house in Hampstead. As he comes in, trying to be quiet, he hears Mrs Kirk call, 'George!'

He goes to her sitting room. Once more a cat leaps from a chair. 'You're late this evening,' she says. 'Philip Bligh rang again. He would like you to ring him back. He left his number. Here, I'll give it to you. Come and sit down for a bit. I had a letter from Andrew today. They think they might come over for Christmas. I'm trying not to get too excited about it. Will you be with your parents? It would be nice if you could meet Andrew.'

This is the way of his world. But this evening he will not stay. 'Will you excuse me? I've got some work to do. The books are in my room.'

Her face shows disappointment. She had wanted a chat.

'Oh. Well, don't forget about poor Philip. Have you eaten yet?'

He lies. 'Yes.'

'I was going to ask you to share my supper.'

'I had something at the Institute.'

'But I thought you said that the restaurant closed at half-past five.'

'I bought some sandwiches.'

He goes up the stairs, clutching a piece of paper on which

she has written the number, knowing that he must not ring Bligh, for it is time to escape before they take him down with them, these old men with their half-forgotten dreams.

I should like to see that boy again, Bligh thinks.

Now that I am back in London we might have dinner together for he needs advice. He seems a strange mixture of the timid and the determined, the definite and the indefinite. But he does not answer my telephone calls. Perhaps the messages are not reaching him. Perhaps that old woman has lost her mind. Well, in the end, what does it matter? There are one or two things I want to do: go to the exhibition of Spanish pictures at the Royal Academy, see the new *Hamlet* at the National, check some references in the library of the Institute and try to find out what Friedrich's new plans for the place are. Yes, there is still much that makes life worthwhile.

So it ends. So Bligh waits and George Loftus never rings back. He realises soon that this is finished and makes no further attempts to get in touch with the boy. He goes to the exhibition, sees the play, visits the Institute and renews his friendship with the librarian, Edith Parr. At the Institute, he asks about George Loftus and is told that he is a small man who works in the department of conservation: shy and dim. Does Bligh want to see him, Edith Parr asks? No, Bligh says, we met once briefly and that is enough; now where are those books? Then he drafts another article for the *Burlington* and calls on the editor who shows interest and is polite. He is invited to dinner parties and to the openings of new galleries and exhibitions where he meets more people and thinks still of the artists of whom they remind him, ranging from his Venetians across Italy, France, Holland, Germany, Europe, the United States, the whole world, until he has a great series of parallels which link the faces of the present to those of the past: a way, he thinks, of defeating time. Occasionally students write to him, perhaps to ask for his memories of Berenson or even of Geoffrey Kirk; as he grows older, Bligh becomes of interest simply as a survivor, a man who has lived through most of the century. Once or twice a year he goes to Cragham to find Bob tormented by deafness and pains in his legs and back, watched over by Beryl who seems ageless, almost glorying in the decrepitude of those around her.

Then he starts to find the stairs to his first-floor flat difficult and has always to take the lift. Now he needs a stick. His eyes begin to fail him and he is grateful for tapes of the spoken word that take the place of books. The young couple in the flat beneath keep an eye on him and call in at odd hours, using the key which he has given them. To the girl, who is called Antonia, he speaks sometimes of the past: of growing up in a cathedral city, of his time in the war, of the world as it used to be, of the holidays at Cragham, sometimes of Catherine ('my friend's wife') whose mystery he wishes no longer to solve, for he fears that the image may break in his head.

His world begins to close in. Bob dies. The funeral is announced as 'private' so Bligh does not go but writes to Charles who acknowledges his letter and hopes he will come again to the house 'even though it is under new management now'. But to move from London is an effort and he does not wish to see the changes that will have been made by Charles's wife Sarah, a keen young girl whom he remembers from one of his last visits before Bob's death. Then Bligh reads in a gossip column in one of the newspapers that Charles, having left the army, is to turn the house into a pleasure park and conference centre; there is, he tells the journalist, 'no alternative, for either we do this or the place will fall down from lack of repair'. The article mentions the history of Cragham, the great wealth of the past, the generals and the Viceroy. Now, it says, the family will move into the stable block.

And George? What happens to George? Well, of course he works on the pictures that he brought back with him. They turn out not to be of great interest, with no evidence in the religious study of the lost Renaissance masterpiece for which he had hoped. He finishes the Dutch landscape first, then the imitation Correggio, then the two hounds and comes last to the portrait of Catherine Layburn which he has left to the end because he fears a renewal of fantasy. Yet as he looks at her face he feels almost nothing: not even curiosity, just a faint regret for a lost time and place. The tear has been mended. All that remains is to inspect the result, arrange for the portrait and the other works to be sent back by carrier, then to tell the accounts department to send Major Layburn a bill.

Is this the end? No, for George there is still the battle between the dreams of Catherine and the dreams of Pat and often these two women seem to tumble over and around each other in his consciousness until he wonders if it will ever be possible to escape from this extraordinary composite creature who descends to fill the long nights. There is also the truth of Pat herself at the reception desk, combing her hair, filing her nails, smiling obligingly at visitors. No, he tells himself, let me comfort the other one: Catherine. Then the next day Pat speaks and he sees some part of her – perhaps her smile or the way she stretches out an arm or stands before him to ask how he is or laughs at his excuse that he is late for an appointment – and this brings the two of them back in this astonishing sequence that seems to be without end. For weeks, for months, this lasts until he begins to fear for his mind.

Then time works its magic and the dreams fade. There is a new girl called Helen in the department of conservation who looks up to George with his superior knowledge and experience and who wishes to make her admiration clear.

He starts to see Helen after work, to continue their discussions about pentimento and the seriousness of flaking, to take her to meet Mrs Kirk. One evening in her room in Highbury, near the Arsenal football ground, they decide to go to bed together in a sensible, matter-of-fact way, and it is fine. She is taller than he is but she does not seem to mind and laughs when he mentions this, saying, 'I hadn't noticed and in any case why should it matter?' Now he knows what ought to come next. He must speak to his parents and arrange to bring Helen to meet them. They will like her. She works and together he and she will earn a reasonable living in the business of pictures and art. At this thought he allows himself a glance backward. Yes, those strange apparently uncontrollable feelings, those fantastic hopes, have gone and it would be foolish to regret their passing, for they had been founded on an unreal view of the world.

NIGEL WATTS

BILLY BAYSWATER

After losing his job on a London building site, young Billy slips
through the social security net. Retarded, disorientated and
destitute, he is as vulnerable to deceit and abuse as he is
responsive to the girl who shows him temporary kindness, and
to the beauty he finds in the parks' trees and flowers. Delight-
ful and devastating by turn, BILLY BAYSWATER draws a
poignant, topical portrait of life for the homeless in the big city,
at times the loneliest place on earth.

'A beautifully crafted imaginative expression of one very
particular view of the world'
The Guardian

'A tremendous imaginative triumph and should be read by
anyone who still thinks that all homeless people are bludgers'
Mary Hope in The Financial Times

'A swelling anger gathers force through the story, made all the
more powerful because of an emotional counter to it, a glorious
sense of humanity and of the city's beauty'
Judy Cooke in The Guardian

'This fine and careful novel about those who live on the margins
of our society is an indictment of that society without saying a
word against it'
Andrew Sinclair in The Times

'I believed in Billy. His fine, highly written story worked very
well. It's very sad and true'
John Healy, author of THE GRASS ARENA

SHUSAKU ENDO

FOREIGN STUDIES

Shusaku Endo, one of Japan's most distinguished and internationally renowned writers, eloquently charts the gulf between East and West in three linked narratives. Evoking Paris in the 1960s, 17th-century Rome and provincial France in the post-war years, he acutely conveys the frustrated alienation felt by three Japanese students when confronted by the spiritual values and culture of Europe.

'Endo to my mind is one of the finest living novelists'
Graham Greene

'Endo has the major novelist's genius for making out of his own and his culture's predicament works of art of wholly universal relevance'
Paul Binding in The Listener

'A writer of remarkable power'
Francis King in the Daily Telegraph

'An immaculate, limpid moral tale, beautifully translated into English'
Mary Hope in the Financial Times

'The whole novel gives a hauntingly authentic feeling of what it is like to be foreign, to be a person apart. Each detail is clearly observed and piercingly true'
Anthony Thwaite in the London Evening Standard

'Quite brilliant'
Ian Rankin in Scotland on Sunday

sceptre

THOMAS KENEALLY

TOWARDS ASMARA

With this powerful and moving novel, Thomas Keneally draws attention to a contemporary issue of global importance: the political causes of famine, exemplified by the long-running Eritrean struggle for independence from Soviet-backed Ethiopia.

Four Westerners travel under Eritrean rebel escort through a land of savage beauty and bitter drought towards the front-line and the ancient capital of Asmara, each one irrevocably changed as they bear witness to the devastation of war as well as to the Eritreans' courage, remarkable organisation and humanity in the face of constant attack.

'Not since FOR WHOM THE BELL TOLLS has a book of such sophistication, the work of a major international novelist, spoken out so unambiguously on behalf of an armed struggle'
The New York Times Book Review

'It is a tribute to the power of his narrative that his book reads as the factual account of a journey behind the lines, in the course of which a forgotten history is given flesh and blood'
The Observer

'Keneally advances on the interminable conflict with all his customary assurance and probing curiosity . . . The war springs vividly to life . . . Keneally keeps things moving through a brilliantly portrayed landscape'
The Guardian

WILLIAM WHARTON

TIDINGS

Deep in the French countryside, Will Kelly and his wife prepare to celebrate thirty years of marriage and Christmas with their four children. With festive boughs of holly and baubles on the tree, Will tries to conjure up the magic of Christmases past but can no longer ignore his fear that this one might be the couple's last. Wryly humorous and piercingly perceptive, this is a moving portrait of family life and of a man striving to understand both his own feelings and those dear to him.

'Wharton's skill is to maintain our sympathy for Will, whilst allowing us to glimpse his unintentional cruelty; and to balance his delicate narrative on the fine line which separates charm from whimsy. His writing is precise, idiosyncratic and perceptive'
Hilary Mantel in the Daily Telegraph

'Wharton may be the only modern writer who can go straight for the heart and make it tick, never more effectively than in this gentle and artfully constructed novel'
Miranda Seymour in the London Evening Standard

'A marvellous recreation of the Christmas spirit and family life, full of the best intentions but fraught always with imminent peril'
Stanley Reynolds in Punch

'A melancholy and beautiful evocation of a dying century'
Nicci Gerrard in The Observer

ROSE TREMAIN

RESTORATION

Winner of the Sunday Express Book of the Year Award
Shortlisted for the Booker Prize

Robert Merivel abandons his medical studies to revel in
gluttony, indolence and buffoonery at the Court of King
Charles II. Finding favour with the King, he serves as 'paper
groom' to the youngest royal mistress in exchange for an
estate and knighthood. But by falling in love with her himself he
violates the rules and is banished from Court. Merivel's
enforced purgatory leads to work in a Quaker Bedlam and a yet
more painful fall from grace before he can achieve spiritual and
social restoration.

Rose Tremain's award-winning novel is a masterful blend of
history and imagination. Rich, humorous and exuberant, but
with a dark undercurrent, RESTORATION's portrait of a past
era suggests telling parallels with the present.

'Daring and sensuous'
Maggie Gee in The Observer

'Robert Merivel is her best creation . . . quite marvellous, a
literary and psychological triumph . . . the book is a *tour de
force*'
Carole Angier in New Statesman & Society

'Comic and profound, subtle and bawdy, utterly relevant to the
present and a masterly portrait of that complex creature, man.
It's a joy to read'
Anne Smith in The Listener

RICHARD WALKER

A CURIOUS CHILD

In a Cairo clinic, Ronny recovers from a sex-change operation. His grandmother, his mother and then Ronny himself sift through their pasts in search of what has led to this bold self-transformation. From decades of Home Counties respectability emerge buried family secrets – of illicit love, thwarted hopes and desires, stifled by conformity and the bonds of duty from which Ronny is breaking free.

'Entirely admirable account of the decline and degeneration of a prosperous, "normal", middle-class English family. The prose is consistently exquisite'
The Times

'Beautifully observed social tragi-comedy . . . the depiction of the older generation's hopes and frustrations is quite remarkable'
Punch

'A remarkably daring first novel'
The Scotsman

'Richard Walker is a master of the time-splicing device . . . an impressive first novel'
The Irish Times

'An intelligent, thought-provoking novel . . . a welcome antidote to all those sweetness-and-light family sagas'
Forum